LADDER UP

Krista Fuller
& Audrey Lincoff

Dedication

To Donna Fuller who always knew this book could be created. While we may have doubted that we could complete the project she was always positive and supportive. Donna was our ultimate coach and fan. Thanks for everything Mom.

Acknowledgements

There are many people with whom this book would not be possible – they are mostly those who have been in our lives for decades or more and have inspired us along the way. They know who they are and we love them dearly.

For this purpose, we want to acknowledge those who went out of their way to help us by giving advice, providing factual information and spending hours reading drafts of the book in various stages; this acknowledgment is for Cate Goethals, Kevin O'Brien, Jim Thomsen, Chris Karam, Badger Godwin, Maura Donaghey, Susan Childers, Keri Robinson, Alan Feldberg, Jason Wister and Elizabeth Kanna.

Prologue

She sat nervously in the chair looking at the reception area with new eyes. Once again, a different person was at the main desk. She could not keep track of everyone who had sat in that chair; she thought that it must be the highest turnover position in the company. Frank, her attorney, was sitting calmly at her side reading the latest version of the company's annual report. She thought she had found the perfect job when she started working here and now she was waiting to meet with the head of Human Resources with her hired attorney.

> A young blonde woman entered the reception area and caught Jane's eye. "You must be Jane Adams. Keith is ready to see you now."

Frank put down the annual report and looked over at Jane to make sure she was ready to go into the meeting.

"Excuse me sir, but this meeting is just between Jane and Keith," she said as she saw Frank standing up and preparing to accompany Jane into the conference room.

"I am not attending this meeting without my attorney, Frank Jenkins," Jane said very decisively. "Keith requested meeting with me and I want Frank with me as my counsel. If that is a problem, we will be happy to leave."

"I need to make sure that Keith has the time to meet with both of you. Please follow me and I will inform him of your presence, Frank."

Jane thought to herself if *Keith wasn't willing to meet with me with Frank in the room, then she would simply see him in court. His decision.*

Jane and Frank followed the receptionist down two flights of stairs and off to the far north corner of the building. Jane thought to herself, *I never even knew this conference room existed all the time that I worked here. One more hidden secret of this corporation.* The receptionist opened the door to the remote room and turned on the lights. Unlike the rest of the conference rooms in the building, this room did not have any windows by the door so interested parties could not happen to glance in to see what was going on inside.

"Take a seat and I will make sure that Keith is available to meet with both of you." As she said this, she exited the room closing the door firmly on her way out.

"Jane, don't worry about this," Frank said reassuringly. "This is usually what happens when I accompany my clients to a meeting with Human Resources. Remember you are doing them a favor by meeting with them ahead of time rather than going directly to the authorities with your findings."

"I understand, but still I never expected it all to end up like this."

"Unfortunately this is what happens when greed and stock options mix with corporate ethics."

After waiting for what seemed like hours, but was probably only 30 minutes, Jane and Frank heard footsteps outside the room. The door opened and in walked two individuals – a tall man wearing a polo shirt and khakis, and a young woman dressed in a skirt and sweater.

"Jane, let me introduce myself. I am Keith Roberts, the head of Human Resources and this is our attorney, Tina Boatwright. When Melissa informed me that Frank was with you today, I felt that Tina should also join in the discussion." As Keith was making these introductions, he moved to take a seat at the head of the conference table.

Frank pulled out business cards and passed them to Keith and Tina. "I am here at Jane's request to support her in her decision about how she wants to go forward with her relationship with your company."

"I understand; and that is why I wanted to meet with Jane face-to-face rather than communicate through e-mail. I am confident that we will be able to work something out today that is satisfactory for both of us."

He is nervous, Jane thought to herself, *quite the opposite of all of the times when I tried to meet with him and he was too busy or was unavailable. He is actually present and focused. It's about time.*

"Jane, you have a long career ahead of you and I am sure that you do not want to be painted as a whistleblower. I am prepared to make you an offer that should be satisfactory to you. In exchange for your nondisclosure of the recent events and agreement and not to enter into legal proceedings against us, the company is prepared to offer you one year of severance pay and a neutral recommendation if you should need it for future employment."

Frank nearly cut him off before he could finish his sentence. "Come on now Keith, you know that a neutral recommendation is required by policy. Please do not lead us to believe that this is a benefit that you are offering to Jane."

"I understand what you are saying Frank." Tina spoke up for the first time probably to insure her job security with Keith. "However, by putting this in writing it supports our commitment to nondisclosure of the recent events."

"What do you mean? The recent events were the company's lack of ethics, not mine," Jane said quite passionately with her voice going up several octaves.

"That is a matter of perspective; however, just to show that we would like this all to go away, if you sign this agreement today, I am prepared to increase the severance package to 18 months," Keith stated quickly and firmly.

Jane thought about her two young children and the fact that her husband had just lost his job. Giving up this package just to fight a case about what was right did not seem worth it to her. She looked at Frank and he seemed to sense her dilemma. "Give Jane and me a moment to discuss your offer."

"Okay. Tina and I will leave and come back here in 30 minutes. Remember the 18 month severance is based on a signing a nondisclosure agreement today." As Keith said this quite firmly, he and Tina stood up and walked quickly out the door.

"Jane you have an excellent case to take to the authorities to make this company accountable for what you have uncovered. You do not need to settle for an 18 month severance package."

"But how long would that take?" Jane asked plaintively. "You know that Jim just lost his job and I do not have any idea as to what the timeline will be for him to find another position. We have the children and a mortgage that was based on both of us working, not both of us being unemployed."

"As I have told you before, the wheels of justice can either move very rapidly or very slowly; I really cannot tell you."

"I think you have told me enough. I have no choice but to accept the offer. It is time for me to forget about this company and to move on with my life."

Chapter 1

Dear Mom and Dad:

Good News- I got the promotion

Bad News- I got the promotion. Now I wish I could crawl under the covers and never go into work.

Love,

Me

My name is Reese Turnbull. Let me tell you the story of my good-news, bad-news message to my parents, Hazel and Wilbert Turnbull, who still live in the same North Dakota town in which they raised me.

How did I get to Seattle? Well, it all started with wanting to get out of Minot and its bitter-cold winters, so I went to college in Bellingham, Washington. I was drawn to the Pacific Northwest, but a big city like Seattle scared me so I settled for living ninety miles north. When not in classes, I worked at

Darcy's. I started as a part-time sales associate at the clothing store but in record time, I was promoted to manager.

The next thing I knew, I had graduated and cast my career lot with Darcy's. The only career advice my parents had ever given me was to pursue whatever my heart desired, as long as it wasn't in retail. They had a photography studio and had been in the retail business their entire lives, so of course they wanted something different for their daughter. Being young and full of myself, I did just the opposite.

Darcy's is headquartered in Seattle. Since Bellingham is only two hours north of Seattle, my store was the test location for new marketing promotions for the chain of stores. As a result, I got to know the head of marketing, Sandy Slaugh. I thought Sandy was everything that I aspired to be but wasn't. At least not yet. She was tall, had perfectly coiffed auburn hair, a creamy complexion and always looked put together. I am seven inches shorter than her in heels, and my dark hair has a mind of its own so I usually have it pulled back into a ponytail.

Sandy came to the store on a Thursday in late September. I thought it would be just another store tour until she asked me to join her for drinks after work. At a nearby pub called Jake's, we ordered Chardonnay and she got to the point.

"Reese, now that you have graduated, what are your plans for the future?" Nothing like being direct. I know you are supposed to be prepared for this question but somehow I never got around to rehearsing for it.

"I never thought I would stay with Darcy's as long as I have; it was just supposed to be a part-time job while I finished my degree in Environmental Studies" is what came out of my mouth.

"The next thing I knew I was promoted to store manager. I discovered that I enjoyed the challenge of management and working in the store. It must be because I always promised myself that I would never work in retail.

"As far as what is next, I really haven't thought a lot about it. I know that I want to stay in the Pacific Northwest and I really want a career."

Sandy was smiling as I was stumbling through my garbled explanation. I made decent money as the manager of the Darcy's department store in Bellingham — decent especially for a twenty-three-year-old, as compared to my college friends who were slogging through temp jobs while moving back in with their parents — but I didn't make Sandy money.

"Let me put it this way," she said after taking a sip of her Pinot Gris. "How far would you like to go in your career?"

I'd never thought about it. But why not? I managed a store, but so had my parents, back in North Dakota. And they'd lost their camera shop in the recession. I loved them but I'd left home for a reason. I wanted a different life. A better life. My own life. I had a good degree and a good job. But I went home alone every night to takeout Chinese and TV marathons. My social life consisted of hot yoga and chilled wine. I wasn't miserable, but I wasn't exactly happy either. I needed a change. But a change to what?

"I honestly don't know," I said, and reached for my own glass of wine before pulling my hand back. "Where is there to go?"

"How about Seattle?" Sandy's eyes bore into mine.

"You mean, corporate?" I realized that I had next to no idea what went on at Darcy's at that level. That is, apart from Sandy's quarterly drop-in visits, and the memos on HR policy and display presentations that I would never admit that I didn't always read.

But my first thought was: that's where Jack is. Jack . . . and Carey.

"You're a good store manager," Sandy was saying. "One of our best, according to the numbers. Sales, rate of returns, customer satisfaction surveys, everything."

"I have a good team," I said, thinking of Michael, my assistant. A guy a few years older than me who was good enough to run a store and never showed any resentment when I was promoted over him. Maybe it was his obvious crush on me, one I wouldn't return even if I could. Maybe that's part of why I needed a change.

"Don't be so modest," Sandy said. "You showed some real initiative. Moving the end-of-summer sales clothes to the front last month wasn't corporate policy. But it worked—those sales went through the roof. And you knew just when to pull it back and put the back-to-school items there. That's more than just being a good corporate soldier, Reese. That's good instinct."

I blushed like a high school freshman on a school-dance date. Or like me after a hug from Jack after a now-rare visit. "Thank you."

"So . . . as you probably know, we have an opening." Sandy's eyes slid to her half-eaten plate of shrimp scampi.

At this point I was ready to chug the rest of my wine; however, my mother's training kicked in and I continued to daintily sip the liquid while I figured out how to respond. My sister told me I could always think on my feet and respond to a statement with no rehearsal, but I definitely did not feel that was the case right now.

"What would I do? Are you sure I would fit in?"

"Reese, you have spunk and moxie, and strong experience working in the field. The office has become too insular and everyone has forgotten that sales occur in the field, not at the corporate office! I would like you to come in as a buying coordinator and learn the buying aspect of the retail

business from the ground up."

Chapter 2

Within days, I was working at the corporate office in Seattle. My move to Seattle was made as painless as possible by my good friend Jack. Jack and I met at Western Washington University. He was two years my senior but from the day that I ran into him (literally) with my Karmann Ghia on campus, we became close friends. I was driving down West Holly Street, looking at sights I normally did not see in Minot, when I gently rear-ended him at a stoplight. Jack came out of his car ready to take me on, but softened in the face of my tears. He is six feet, four inches with the greenest eyes you have ever seen, but he had—and still has—a girlfriend. Jack and Carey and I became close friends. This will always disappoint me a little because he is someone of whom my father would approve – a rare occurrence in my life.

After graduation, Jack and Carey moved to Seattle. Jack joined an architectural firm, and Carey works part-time while waiting to get a job with the Seattle Police Department.

They were excited about my move to the big city and helped me find a great loft apartment in the Pioneer Square area of the city. Pioneer Square is right next to downtown Seattle and is one of the oldest parts of the city. It is made up of warehouses and old brick buildings that are gradually being converted to affordable apartment living. Full of music clubs and cobblestone streets, it is where musicians from Ray Charles and Quincy Jones to Jimi Hendrix and Kurt Cobain had their first professional gigs.

My loft apartment, eight hundred square feet, is above an Italian restaurant named Carmine's. This location is both bad and good—the wonderful smells from the restaurant are bad for a diet, but Chef Carmine took a liking to me and I always have access to a hot meal and great wine.

My apartment is one big room with one wall that has floor-to-ceiling windows that allows me to look out at the shipyards on Puget Sound. Jack helped me break up the room into sections, using my furniture to create a cozy living space. The only unfortunate area in the apartment is the bathroom. It was added by the landlord so he could rent the space and as a result, it is super tiny. To call it closet-size would be generous. Literally, if you are in the bathroom, you have to move to the side to open the door. And the pipes are noisy, and leak now and then. But the location, the view and the economical rent make it all worthwhile.

On October 15, I started my new job at headquarters as the buying coordinator. Sandy introduced me to the buying team: Jason, a recruit from a major department store with ten years of retail buying experience; Christine, a newly minted MBA with a specialty in marketing from Wellesley College; and Sarah, the original buyer for Darcy's. Sarah thought she should have had Sandy's job and felt passed over when Sandy came on board a year ago.

The entire team collected in the marketing conference room for the big introduction. I felt like I was a new animal in the zoo with all of the eyes on me. "Team, I want you to meet Reese. I know that you all know the great job she has done for Darcy's in her past role as the manager of our test location in Bellingham. We are lucky that she has agreed to make the move to Seattle. I will leave it to each of you to introduce yourselves and tell her how she can be of assistance to you."

Sarah was the first to speak up. "Thank goodness we will finally have some administrative help. I have two months' worth of expense reports that I will give you to process for me."

Sandy jumped in before I could speak. "Sarah, I did not bring Reese here to be your admin. She is here to give us insight on what really goes on in the stores so that we can make our buying more relevant to our customers." She walked out of the room, and Sarah followed. Everyone else looked at their phones to see when their next meeting was scheduled.

Sarah followed Sandy out of the room to try to clarify what she meant by her comment about me.

Christine put down her phone. "Well, I have ten minutes before I start back-to-back meetings, so what do you need from me, Reese?"

"If you could just show me where my desk is, that would be helpful," I said timidly.

Jason spoke up. "There is a vacant cubicle by me and I am sure that Sandy would be okay with you taking that spot. Come with me and I will show you your new living quarters."

Jason is short and looks like he has never missed a meal. He's not really the type you'd expect to be in the buying department of a clothing retailer. As we walked to the cubicle area he shared with me how he came to Darcy's. "I was stuck in a rut in my last job and was looking for a company that had the potential for growth. I am originally from New York but after moving out here with my family for my last job, I did not want to have to relocate them again. I have two boys who are ages five and seven, and they are just starting school."

Jason showed me the one vacant cubicle, in the darkest corner of the office. I could see why no one had claimed it; it was so far away from the windows and natural light that you could grow mushrooms in the space.

"I know this is less than an optimal location but at least you will be out of the view of Sandy and the other executives when they come down the hall," Jason said. "Take it from me, you want to be in a low-profile spot when sales are not performing at the forecasted levels," he said. "Sorry, but it hasn't been dusted since Jane left the company."

I'd had enough for one day, but made a mental note to ask him about Jane. I had never heard of Jane and it seemed a little mysterious.

Jack, Carey and I like to have dinner together and solve all of the problems of the world, so I was happy to spend the evening with them after my first day. Carey was a fantastic cook and loved to experiment with new recipes, and tonight she was making Chicken Cordon Bleu.

"So you think Christine is stuck up, Jason is in over his head, and Sarah is not to be trusted." As usual, Jack had listened to all of my ramblings and was able to summarize my thoughts in as few words as possible.

"Yes, that is my first impression. I am really not sure why Sandy has transferred me to Seattle." I sipped my wine. "I know she doesn't want me to be an administrative clerk but I am really not sure what she wants me to do."

Our conversation was interrupted as Carey called me to the table and Jack poured each of us another glass of Viognier.

"Guys, I can't eat like this every night," I said, "or I will need to buy a new wardrobe."

"Don't worry. We can't afford this level of eating either but we wanted to do something special for your very first day. Now let's get back to planning how you should handle your new position. In a perfect world, what would you want to do with this position?" Carey set down her glass and stared at me.

"I think that the company has lost contact with its customers. Darcy's was created to provide inexpensive clothes for customers primarily located in small towns. This is my background from growing up in North Dakota. Just because we lived five hours from a major city, we still wanted to be able to buy fashionable clothes at a reasonable price. In the past year the clothes seem to be poorly made and the styles are out of date before they hit the stores. The only reason that sales have not suffered to a greater extent is that the customer does not have any other local option—but ultimately, if we're not giving the customer what they want, they'll get it somewhere else. I think this is why Sandy has brought me to the corporate office and especially why she wants me to work in the buying department."

"That makes sense," Carey said. "It would also explain why your new locations are based in relatively small towns rather than in urban locations. It looks like the first thing you need to do is figure out who is really making the decisions regarding the inventory that is being bought for the stores. You have only been there one day so don't expect to have all of the answers tonight. Now let's finish off this wine, since we know it will never be as good as it is right now."

Jack topped off my glass and we began discussing his latest project, which was developing a low-cost model for a new elementary school to be built in West Seattle.

Chapter 3

Much to my surprise, Christine was also present for my 8 a.m. meeting with Sandy.

"Now that you are here, Reese, I want to discuss what we need to accomplish. As you know, we need to send out all of the holiday promotion materials next week. The mock store is already set up, and I would like you and Christine to review the prototype before the executives tour the location at 4:00 this afternoon. If something is not right I expect you to fix it so that we do not have any controversy when Clark—the CEO—and Bill—the Head of Operations—are giving us their final approval."

Christine shot me a quick glance. "Sandy, as you know, I have overseen everything so far regarding these promotions. I really do not know what you expect from bringing Reese into the decision matrix so late in the process."

"Christine, the reason Reese is here is to bring a field perspective to our overall merchandising strategy. I am sure what you have done is excellent. But I will feel more comfortable once we have a field perspective of the merchandising concept."

"I understand. Come on, Reese. I have thirty minutes right now to review the promotional materials with you." It was clear that Christine wasn't interested in dealing with this. I didn't expect her to get so frustrated with me just for trying to make her promotion more successful. Her face showed absolute disgust at having to take the time to talk to me. Good information for me for the future.

I did not even know that there was space available for us on the second floor. Our headquarters are in an old warehouse that was located next to the ship yards and railroad tracks. The company started with renting space on the 8th floor and as the company has expanded, we have taken over more space. It is rumored that due to the strange layout of the warehouse space, individuals have been lost for hours trying to go from one department to the next. The last thing I wanted to do was get lost in this building trying to find the prototype space on the 2nd floor. I hastily got up from my seat and followed Christine out of Sandy's office.

Christine did not even look at me as she scurried towards the stairs to the elevator. She raced down three flights of stairs and then veered off to get on an elevator to the second floor. I just barely got in the door before she jabbed at the button for the second floor. "I can't believe Sandy is making me show you this prototype. I have already had every department in the building review it, including the asset protection group (that is our fancy word for the security department)!"

When the doors opened, she darted forward to punch a key code into a closed room in the bowels of the building. Inside was warehouse space with a mock store outfitted for the holiday season. The colors were red, white and silver with streams of tinsel flowing everywhere.

My impression was that this looked great, but that hanging tinsel would be too time-consuming and complicated in a real store. The store managers would never have the time or staff to artfully put the tinsel in the exact placement that Christine had outlined.

"How do you expect the stores to put up this tinsel?" I said. "In the past, you sent a package with an instruction book and then the stores followed those instructions. I am curious as to how they will know how to put up all this tinsel."

"That is simple. We will just post a video of this store and all store employees can watch the video, and then follow the directions."

"So you have figured out how to get the video feed to work so that one thousand locations can actually watch the program?"

"Of course. Stop being such a negative personality."

I had no reply. She obviously did not want to hear a word that I had to say.

"Are you done looking at the store yet?" Christine looked at her phone. "I really have a meeting I must get to and I don't have time to waste with you at this site."

I tried to ignore the insult. "Why don't you go on to your meeting, and I will spend some time here becoming familiar with your plans."

"Do what you want." She turned and I almost missed the roll of her eyes, which did not surprise me. "I know I have such a great rapport with Clark and Bill that the walk through this afternoon will be perfect."

With that, she walked out of the room.

I now had a problem. There was no way that this merchandising program could be executed in the field and Sandy had told us to fix it before the tour. Christine obviously was oblivious to what it took to accomplish anything at the store level and if I did not do something about this problem, Sandy would regret her decision to bring me to Seattle.

I began pulling down the reams of tinsel. As soon as I was done, I could actually see the merchandise. Not just silky flash.

I now knew what the prototype should look like. But I had to be careful to not go too far and risk having Christine biting my head off. I hastily left the room and ran up the stairs to my remote cubicle. I wanted to talk about this problem with Jason.

"So," he said with a smile, "you had the audacity to tell Queen Christine that her promotion would not work."

"Well, I tried," I said, "but then she called me negative and totally shut down on me. I think her promotion materials are fine, but the tinsel-hanging will not be executed with any degree of consistency in the field and the stores will look terrible."

"I think you have to say just that during the walk-through," Jason said, rubbing his chin. "Go back to the site and put the tinsel back up. Then when the walk-through is taking place, you can remove it and show the executives an alternate plan. Remember that when you are new, it is the best time to get them to listen to you."

How easy it was for Jason to say this. He wouldn't even be there. But I had to admit what he said did make sense.

By three thirty I had all of the tinsel back in place. The entire buying team was nervously waiting for the arrival of the executives who would approve—or not approve—the launch of the promotional materials. Christine had gone home during the day and changed into an A-line black skirt and a crème-colored blouse that was going to be heavily promoted on the merchandising displays. I had to admit this looked a lot better than the black slacks and red turtleneck top that I had been wearing all day as I took down and rehung tinsel. At 3:55 on the dot, two men came into the room, discussing an upcoming basketball game. Obviously everyone at the corporate headquarters came to all the meetings early. Definitely something I was going to have to work on.

Clark is about fifty-five, with receding dark hair and coal-brown eyes that make you feel that you are the only thing that he sees. Bill is a tad younger than Clark, tall and skinny, and always in motion. I knew Bill from his store tours in Bellingham. Rumor has it he does store tours so that he can get away from Clark and the corporate environment.

"Reese, it is great to see you," Bill said, and introduced me to Clark.

"Nice to see you again, Reese." Clark's eyes barely met mine. "Now, Sandy, what do we have here for our promotion for holiday? You know that sales have been soft and we need an impactful holiday promotion to save our sales forecast for the year."

Sandy nodded to Christine, who moved up to the front of the group and began her pitch. "Notice how we are focusing on the hot items that we received from our manufacturer overseas. This will ensure that not only will we have the latest fashions, but that we will be able to generate the most revenue from our sales. It will be necessary for all of the stores to follow these directions exactly to reap the most benefit from this promotion."

As Christine spoke, I saw Bill walk away from the group and start to play with the tinsel. "All of this tinsel reminds me of the Christmas trees my family decorated when I was a child. I remember how we would put the tinsel on in clumps and have tinsel fights. Mom had to come back and re-hang all the tinsel strand by strand."

"Reese, I hear what Christine is saying regarding the field needing to execute this perfectly," Clark said. "What is your impression as to whether or not they will be able to do this?"

My stomach churned as all eyes turned to me. Sandy was standing in the back ground with her arms crossed and Christine was sending me dagger looks. Clark had 100 percent of his attention on me.

"I think the items that are being promoted are great. Everyone knows the creamy white tops like the one Christine is wearing are a hit at Christmas time."

"But what about the promotional materials?" Clark was not going to let me off the hook.

"Well," I said, "like Bill said when he was talking about his family Christmas tree, hanging tinsel could be problematic. I would suggest that you save the tinsel for the ten key stores located in urban areas where they have enough staff to execute it correctly. The rest of the fleet could eliminate the tinsel and replace it with silver stars positioned by the key elements."

Sandy looked at me and smiled from the back of the room. I knew then that she saw the problem originally but did not know how to handle Christine, so she used this as a test of my diplomacy.

Christine jumped in. "You know, Clark, when you and I discussed your vision for this promotion you specifically said you wanted the stores to shine."

"I may have said that, Christine. However, I did not want to give something to the stores that would be too difficult to execute. I agree with Reese's suggestion, so let's do it, and end the discussion. I want these materials sent out by the end of the week." He turned and made for the door with Bill on his heels.

Chapter 4

The rest of us stood there in silence, although I was positive they all could hear my heart beating out of my chest. Slowly, we filed out of the room. Christine followed Sandy to the elevator, but I took the stairs and walked back to my dark cube.

"What happened down there, Reese?" asked Jason. "It was dead silent when Christine and Sandy came back upstairs."

"Well, despite my flight instinct, I stood my ground with Bill's help." I told Jason about Bill's childhood memory. "I took that lead and told the group that the stores would look inconsistent if we tried to have them execute the planned promotion."

Jason's eyes were wide open. "Tell me more."

He continued to smile as I went on. And then it occurred to me that I had no idea what would happen next. With that, I tried to find Christine and Sandy to ask, but their offices were empty and dark.

"Reese, go home and forget about it," Jason said. "I'm sure Sandy already has a plan in mind that she'll share with us tomorrow. She knows how important this holiday season is to our bottom line."

"Jason, it's very different in the stores. We were a team and always came together to solve things. As the face to the customer, we didn't like to leave loose ends."

Jason shook his head. "Reese, it is different here, and you'll learn to adapt. You're smart and remember that you've been brought here to help us. But it will take time for you to know how to navigate the corporate waters. It's your first week, your first holiday at corporate, and we've had soft sales. Give yourself a break." And with that, he wished me a nice evening, put on his jacket and headed for the elevator.

It suddenly became very dark. It was past six and everyone had gone home. As store manager, I was usually the last one to leave. And as the newbie in corporate, I still was. Another thing to which I'd adapt, I hoped.

I wandered around the hallway with my phone as a flashlight until I found the light switch. I just hoped that I'd remember to turn them off when I left.

I sat and checked my email. There were messages from the Bellingham store employees, congratulating me on my promotion. It was really nice of people to care, but I had no idea how they even knew. Then I saw the announcement that someone from HR had written about me at the bottom of one of their emails. Curious.

But nothing from Christine or Sandy.

When I got to my building, I peeked inside Carmine's to see if my chef buddy was around. I guess he could read my expression as he said, "Reese, you look like a deer in the headlights. Sit down, I'll pour you a glass of wine and we'll talk."

I did as he said. "Just one glass and only if you'll feed me. After all, it's a school night and work is a little crazy right now." But after a big sip of the amazing Chianti, I finally felt like I could breathe again.

And then the floodgates opened. "I don't even know where to start. When I was managing the store in Bellingham, I knew what I was doing. We were a team. When there were issues, we discussed them. We knew our job was to put the customer first and make our sales goals, and we had to work together to be successful. Since the minute I was introduced to my new team in Seattle, I feel like it's upside down and people only care about their own success. What..."

Carmine interrupted me and said, "Reese, slow down. Take a deep breath and please eat your pasta while it's hot." I obliged, because my stomach was growling as it occurred to me that I hadn't had time for lunch before the walk through."

"I'll let you tell me what happened but first I want you to listen to me while you eat. In this restaurant, I hear all sorts of stories from my regulars. I know where they work, what their day is like and the challenges they face at work, how they want to move up and when they do, how hard it is."

I felt like he was my dad about to tell me to grow up, but I listened, drank more wine and finally started to eat my dinner.

"What you're going through is normal and the key is how you deal with it. Things don't just happen; there is always a strategy in play when it comes to business. But people need strategies, too, if they're going to survive and thrive."

My glass was empty and Carmine pulled the bottle off the shelf to pour me more. "C, I can't have a second glass—it's a school night!" But he poured it anyway and I drank.

"Everybody needs a mentor—someone who will give you guidance and provide a safe place for you to talk things through. You need to find that person, carefully of course. But despite your drive and quick advancement in the company, you can't do it alone."

With my mouth full of pasta, he continued, "You are smart, young and stubborn, Reese. And also a little naïve, which is part of your charm. We've all been there and think we will be different, that we'll change things. Maybe you can, but don't count on it. So now tell me the whole story."

I told Carmine all about the walk-through in great detail, sipping what seemed to be a bottomless glass of wine. He listened intently, which I appreciated. The restaurant was quiet now and I realized we'd been sitting there for more than two hours. "C, it's getting late and I need to get home. Thanks for listening and for the great advice. I'll think about it."

As I walked out, I did a little window shopping to get some fresh air and when I walked into my loft, I realized I'd had more wine than I should have. "Great," I muttered to myself. Then the phone rang. I figured it was Jack or Carey, so I let it go to voicemail.

But as I got into my PJs, I thought I'd better listen to the message. "Reese, this is Sandy. Be in my office at seven a.m. sharp for a team meeting. We need a plan for the promotion so we can ship on Friday."

Beep. She did not sound pleased.

It was now past eleven and my mind was racing. "Did I do the right thing?" I asked out loud. How would Christine react to this meeting? And would Jason and Sarah sit quietly, or actually help?

I tried to sleep, but the wine and fear were a bad combination. When the alarm rang at five thirty, I felt as if I hadn't slept a wink. And I looked like it, too. "Thanks,

Carmine," I whispered as I rolled my eyes. But I knew I only had myself and my immaturity to blame.

It was still dark outside but daybreak was near. I thought a walk to work—fresh air—would help clear my head. At six thirty, I was in the coffee shop at the basement of Darcy's when Christine walked in. Just as I thought I'd escaped her line of sight, she sat down right next to me.

"Hello, Reese," she said. "You're here early, but I can understand if you're concerned about today's meeting and couldn't sleep." Christine was her flippant self; not much had changed from yesterday.

Before I could respond, she continued in a stern voice. "I think the tinsel promotion would have worked fine in all stores. You were able to rehang all the tinsel before the walk-through, so how hard can it be? And we could have told the stores to do it after hours. Clark has made up his mind, but he'll see what a mistake it was when the season is over. The stores won't look festive and customers will shop elsewhere. After all, this is the time for holiday spirit and cheer."

With that, she gave me a glare, picked up her coffee and left me sitting with my coffee getting cold, and my mind riddled with fear.

Chapter 5

Jason was waiting for me in my cube. No *Good morning*, just straight to the point. "What is going to happen in this meeting?" Then he took a deep breath and said, "And you don't look so hot. What's wrong?"

"Jason, I hardly slept because I heard Sandy's message after way too much wine. I saw Christine this morning and she's on a tear. She explained. "Christine blames me for this and I feel as if I'm now enemy number one. I did what I knew was right and Clark agreed. I'm sure Sandy will have Christine be in charge, so we'll just have to take orders from her and try not to explode."

It was nearly 6:50 a.m. but I didn't want to be the last one to get to Sandy's office, so I grabbed Jason's arm and said, "Let's go."

"Reese, I'll meet you in there. I need to go call my wife and wake her up. I had to leave so early and I forgot to reset her alarm."

I walked toward Sandy's office and saw that the door was closed. I knocked, but got no answer. I waited a minute and as I went to knock again, Christine burst out of Sandy's office, nearly bowled me over, and turned toward her office. Her hands were full of papers and files, and she was having a hard time juggling them. All I could think of was: *not good*.

I walked into Sandy's office and she greeted me blankly. "Good morning, Reese. Thank you so much for being here this early. We have a lot to get done in the next thirty minutes, so as soon as the others get here, we'll get started."

What came out of my mouth was, "You're welcome." In walked Christine. I could tell from her expression that she thought we were talking about Clark's comments during the walk-through, because she glared at me, eyes rolling, as if to say *Thanks for nothing*.

Jason and Sarah followed closely behind and shut the door.

"Team, we have a big hurdle to overcome after yesterday's walk-through," Sandy began. "I spoke with Clark and Bill last night, and they're very concerned about our ability to execute."

Christine was on pins and needles at this point. "Well Sandy, we should have just left things as they were. I personally don't like my credibility being questioned, especially with my experience."

"Christine, this is not personal. We are doing the right thing for our store employees. I was asked to figure out how to bolster holiday sales, so I felt that information from the front line would help. I spent the last several months touring stores and talking to employees, and I learned a lot. It's why I decided to bring the front-line experience to our team. It's why I hired Reese."

Christine was seething. "Now I'm confused. Why didn't we know this? We could have thought these same things through if we'd known there were problems."

"Christine, I felt that I needed to think outside the box. You don't have field experience so I wouldn't have expected you to bring that perspective. Now can we please move on," Sandy said, in a measured and patronizing tone.

Dead silence. Just like after the walk-through. I really didn't know what to do or where to look, so I looked down at my notebook.

Sandy stood up and walked over to her whiteboard. "Reese, you're on. What do we need to do to get materials ready for Friday?"

I was visibly flustered and Christine could see it. For the first time today, I caught her little grin. *Great*, I thought. I was not prepared to be asked this question, and I felt as if I'd forgotten everything I recommended the day before.

All eyes turned to me. "Well, we need a plan."

"Yes, Reese. I'm asking you to lead that exercise so we have it when this meeting adjourns in twenty-two minutes." She sounded none too pleased. "We are all here to support and execute, and I'll remain point to Clark and Bill. But you are the lead."

I took a deep breath and walked over to the whiteboard. "We have to write instructions for hanging the silver stars for all stores that will use them. We don't have enough time to create a video and I don't think we need one. We also need to review the video for tinsel-hanging to make sure it applies to only the ten stores that will actually hang tinsel. We will need to work with IT to ensure they have the correct list of stores receiving the video so they're enabled..."

Sandy was writing this all on the whiteboard in a column on the left, leaving the column on the right for assigning tasks.

I continued, "We need the mailroom to be prepared to make copies of the star instructions and they also need to be prepared to mail two types of packages."

As I said this, it occurred to me that I didn't even know what the mailroom did, who made copies, and how it might work. I was just using what I knew from the stores. It was an assumption I'd soon regret.

"Well," Christine barked, "that's not how it works around here when we change things last-minute. We'll have to make the copies and prepare materials for mailing now."

"Christine is right, Reese," said Sandy. "The mailroom brings in extra help to prepare promotions for mailing, but we already did that. We don't have a budget to get temp help in now and we don't have the time. It's going to be a busy few days but we have no choice."

"Okay, Sandy, I understand. I guess I'm just used to how the stores work and I—"

"Well, now you know. You should always ask first because it's different here than in the stores. Christine, I'm going to ask you to write a draft of the instructions for the stores using stars and then run it by Reese to ensure it makes sense for how the stores operate. Jason, please work with IT to make sure they prepare the ten stores for video instructions. Reese, please review the video and all other instructions for those ten stores.

"Sarah, please alert the mailroom and work with them to figure out what we need to do get the two mailings out on Friday. I also want you to make sure there will be four available copiers, with paper, that you can use.

"Reese and Christine, I expect a final version of the instructions for stores using the stars on my desk before you leave tonight so I can review it first thing in the morning. I also want to review the instructions for the stores using tinsel. I'll commit to returning feedback by noon tomorrow so you can copy and assemble the mailing for Friday's noon mailing deadline."

"It is now seven thirty and I have another meeting to get to. You can use my office to align."

I completed the whiteboard with the list of assignments and turned to the team, trying to channel my best managerial skills. "I am really going to need your help to get this done correctly. We are a team with a common goal, to ensure we make—"

Christine interrupted. "We get it, Reese. We all know you ran the store. It's different here but we have to get this done or my promotion will fail. Team, let's get moving now. Reese, I'll let you know when I have something for you to review. To be honest, I'm not sure why I even have to write this instead of you." And as she finished her last word, she was out the door.

Jason looked at me in disbelief. "Great. Here I thought we were done and now it's crunch time again. I sure hope you know what you're doing. I'll be down at IT."

Sarah said nothing and left the room, but her look spoke volumes. I walked back to my cube. It was not even 8 a.m., my coffee was as cold as my teammates, and I was no longer the shiny, new kid.

Chapter 6

I worked furiously to review the video and other materials for the ten stores that would still merchandise with tinsel. I even went down to the second floor to validate the steps. I also wanted to familiarize myself with anything else that would be helpful so I didn't make bad assumptions again. When I looked at the clock on my computer I realized it was almost noon and I'd had nothing from Christine. How hard could it be to write simple instructions, especially when you had a set of instructions for tinsel and this was less complicated? She must have heard my thoughts because the next thing I knew, she was hovering.

"Are you done with your review of the video, Reese? If you're ready, we can sit down and review what I've done for the other stores."

"Christine, thanks so much. I think it might be easier if I read through things on my own. I'm visual and will want to actually use the instructions downstairs to make sure they're sound. Can we meet at three p.m. to discuss?"

"Well, if you must, go ahead. I have an appointment outside of the office and will be back around three thirty. I think what I've prepared is just fine. See you then." She took off in a huff.

I went across the street to grab a quick sandwich and then came back to my desk. About halfway through the instructions, I decided to go down to the second floor instead. I was just about to escape when Jason descended on me. "Reese, I spoke with IT and I think they understand what we're doing, although some stores may still receive a reminder to download the video even though they're not hanging tinsel. We won't know for sure until we do our mailing. We could send an email to all of those stores to tell them to ignore the reminder if they get it."

"I don't want to send an email to that many stores unnecessarily," I told him. "It's about to be their busiest time and it will just confuse them. I think we should trust that IT will get it right and be prepared to deal with any star stores that get the reminder."

"Okay. Then I think my work is done." And with that, he walked away. It struck me as odd that he didn't ask if I needed any other help, but I let it slide.

I used the stairs to get to the second floor and discovered that the room was locked. It took a while, but I found someone with the code to open the door and finally got inside. For the next two hours, I edited and hung stars, and then realized it was four p.m.

I got back to my desk to see a note from Christine: *I'm in my office when you're ready*. I thought this was a good sign.

I was motioned into Christine's office and sat there while she finished up a phone conversation that seemed far too personal for my ears. "Sorry, Reese, but I had to take care of something important. Are you ready to walk me through your changes?"

"Well, I can, but my changes are minor. I really want to get this to Sandy, so what if I leave you a copy and you go over it when you can. I don't really have any questions for you." Apparently, that didn't sit well.

"Fine. If you think it's ready for Sandy, then take it to her. If I would have known you were going to do that, I wouldn't have rushed back."

Yeah, right. Rushed back? "Christine, I'm sorry. You said you'd be back so I..." But she'd dismissed me by turning to her back desk and unwrapped the huge Prada bag she had clearly just purchased. *How does she find the time and money to shop for things like this,* I wondered as I left her office.

In Sandy's office, she asked for the two sets of materials and grilled me about their content. "Yes," I said, "I promise they are sound and ready for your eyes. I even went to the second floor to test them out."

"Well I have high expectations, since you've been in the stores, so I'll read them through that lens. Now have you checked in with Jason and Sarah?"

"I have spoken with Jason and will go to Sarah next."

"I suggest you go find her now."

Halfway down the hall, I realized that I hadn't told her about Jason's concerns with IT, but decided to let it go for now. It had been a long day and there was still a lot to get done tomorrow to make our deadline.

I caught Sarah at the elevator. She was a single mom who left promptly at five p.m. each night to pick up her twins from day care. Apparently there is a hefty fee for every minute after they close and Sarah had to get to Redmond to retrieve them.

"Sarah, are we ready to start copying tomorrow afternoon?"

"Reese, I think so, but won't know until tomorrow morning."

At this point I wasn't sure if she was just disinterested or actually trying to derail things, but I took the high road and said OK. "Just be sure that we are ready to go with four copiers at one p.m. sharp. It's going to take a long time to copy the materials and assemble them, and I don't want us to be here all night."

"Reese, you know I have to leave by five p.m. Sorry," she said with a trailing voice as the elevator door closed behind her.

As I went back to my desk to collect my thoughts, I considered telling Sandy about the potential issues we were having. But her door was closed and I took it to mean that she wanted privacy. I was exhausted and hungry, but decided to go to my regular Wednesday night yoga class anyway. I was new and wanted to make some friends, which would be great.

It took me most of the class to finally relax and stop thinking about work. And, while struggling to get into the tree pose, I noticed the cutest guy in front of me. I always have trouble holding my balance when I have to stand on only one leg, but this guy was amazing. He just crossed his right leg over his left and his foot literally was touching his hip. He did not even sway as he accomplished it.

After class, I gathered my things and I noticed that the cute guy was sitting on the bench putting on his shoes. I walked over to him to strike up some sort of a conversation.

"You were amazing, the way you executed tree pose." Not the most original pickup line, but at least I was trying. Carey and Jack would be proud.

He looked up at me as if to see who would think doing something as basic as a tree pose was amazing. "Thanks, but since I have been practicing yoga for over five years, some of these poses are pretty basic to me. I've noticed you in the class the past couple of weeks. I'm Dan. And you are?"

Yay, mission accomplished. I have his name. "Mine is Reese and I just moved here this past month. I really haven't been practicing yoga very long, but this place is close to my apartment and I wanted to check it out."

"The longer you stick with yoga the more you will enjoy it. A group of us are going out for burgers. Do you want to come along?"

I just wanted to get home and crawl into bed but I was starving. "I'll walk with you but I'm going to take mine to go. Today was a long day and tomorrow could be, too."

I joined Dan and two other women from our class. I was focused on Dan, as he was just my type: athletic, with a great smile and dark hair.

"What are you doing in Seattle, Dan?" I wanted to keep the conversation going.

"I am currently finishing my law degree and working part-time at a law office. I have lived in Seattle my whole life, and I am trying to work and go to school so that when I graduate I will not be overwhelmed with debt."

"Wow. With all of that going on I am surprised you take the time for yoga."

"Yoga is what keeps me sane. You have to maintain a work-life balance in this crazy city or you will end up like some wild person running in circles."

With that encouraging or depressing statement, our food was delivered. "Great meeting you, Reese," Dan said. "See you next week." And with that, I walked home.

I ran up the stairs to my loft, dropped my yoga mat and stood at the counter while I scarfed my burger. I was bound and determined to crawl into bed and get a good night's sleep so I'd be ready to lead the charge in the morning, which would come way too fast.

Chapter 7

Surprisingly enough, the next two days, while longer than we wanted them to be, flew by. We brought donuts to the mailroom, and the employees there worked extra hard to meet the mailing deadline. I felt as if I'd been hit by a train and when I reached my front door on Friday night, immediately donned my PJs and crashed on the couch.

When I woke up sometime around midnight, I brushed my teeth and crawled into bed. It was noon on Saturday when the phone woke me up! I was supposed to meet Jack and Carey that afternoon to Christmas-shop and apparently I was late. I rallied, looking like a train hit me, but we had a successful and busy day. We stopped for pizza and wine on our way home, enjoying the tailgate parties lining Pioneer Square in anticipation of the Seahawks game the next day.

After all of the craziness to get the promotion to the stores, Monday morning was eerily quiet in the corporate office—so the opposite of the store atmosphere. People came in later, left early and seemed to be jovial. Even Christine was in a great mood, inviting us to a holiday team lunch on that Friday. I thought it odd that Sandy wasn't the one to set it up, but I figured that Christine was told to do it. It was actually kind of fun, although I did not have wine with the rest of the team. My dad always told me to never drink at lunch—and if at an evening work function, drink white wine that I could dilute with water. It was Friday afternoon and the wine could wait.

Despite my mom's pleas, I decided to stay in Seattle for the holidays. The city was really festive with all the lights and decorations, and I wanted to enjoy my new life a bit. Mom and Dad were disappointed, but I think they were also relieved that I was creating a life of my own in the big city.

We were now in the third week of the promotion and sales were slightly exceeding our goals. "Phew," I thought and then said out loud in my cube.

Jason overheard me and said, "Reese, it looks like the change in the promotion didn't hurt sales. Great job. You're safe from Christine's ire for a while."

"Jason, I had to do the right thing. And really, it's the merchandise that has to sell. It sounds as if our pricing is helping more than tinsel and stars, but I'll take the safety net if you think so!"

"I think that's wise," he said. As he got up to go to lunch, he added: "I'm not sure what you're doing for the holidays, but my wife and I are having a small gathering this weekend and you're more than welcome to come. I know she's anxious to meet you."

"I'd love to, thanks so much." And with that, he was out the door.

The party was fun although odd, as I was the only one from work who was there. I was not sure why, but decided not to ask. It was just a little awkward and I just hoped he wouldn't bring up the party at work on Monday.

The weeks of Christmas and New Year's, while lots of fun, went way too quickly. I walked all over downtown, even to the Space Needle, to see the decorations in store windows. I loved the trees in the Fairmont Hotel and persevered to stay in the line at the Sheraton to see the gingerbread houses. I even stopped for a glass of wine at The Pink Door, which has amazing views of Elliott Bay and West Seattle. As I stood in front of the Carousel on Westlake, I felt like a kid in a candy store and that all the work craziness was worth it.

Jack and Carey joined me at Carmine's for New Year's Eve dinner. Of course, C set us up with a dinner that was amazing. He sat with us as the year turned over, toasting with bubbly to a new year filled with success, laughter and love. It was a good thing we all lived within walking distance, too!

I walked upstairs with air under my feet. I had a feeling that next year was going to be the best ever and I couldn't wait.

Chapter 8

Carey and I decided that before getting back to the swing of things post-holiday, we needed to make a quick trip back up to Bellingham and stop in at all of our old haunts. We both had Saturday and Sunday free so we piled into my Karmann Ghia and left Jack behind to have a girl's weekend up North. We were lucky the weather, while grey and foggy, was not cold and we did not have any snow or ice to deal with as we made the drive north on I-5.

"I think this is the year that I will get accepted into the Police Academy." Carey stated with New Year's optimism. "They are really focusing on bringing new blood into the force and I have been training nonstop so that I will pass the initial physical."

"Are you really sure this is what you want to do? With all of the challenges that have gone on in the department over the past year I was hoping that you had given up on this idea."

"Reese, my entire family has worked in law enforcement and I want to prove to my brothers and Dad that I can serve as well as they can. My true goal would be to put in the time on patrol level and then to be promoted to the rank of detective. Blame it on all my years of reading Nancy Drew mysteries, but I really would like to solve real world crime."

"You know life in books always makes it look so simple; however, in the real world things aren't usually so glamorous or cut and dried." I responded sagely. "I know just from my first weeks working in the corporate office that there are more hidden agendas with people than anyone can come close to keeping track of."

"I get it but still this is my dream and I have to go for it." With that explanation I decided once again it was time to drop the topic of joining the Police Department and instead focus on the traffic as we entered Bellingham.

Our first stop was our old hang out Jake's. I had an immediate flash back to the meeting I had with Sandy here just nearly four months ago. " I know that I said that I was not going to talk about work on this trip, however since we are right next door to my old store do you mind stopping in so that I can say 'hi' to the staff."

"Of course not. Just promise we'll only spend 30 minutes there and that you won't jump in and decide to help everyone out by running the cash register."

"I promise it is just to say 'hi'. "

We settled our bill with Jake and then walked two blocks over to the Darcy's location. When I walked into the store I immediately sensed that something was wrong. There was a line of customers at the customer service desk and voices were raised so that everyone could tell that something was not right.

I saw my old assistant manager, Tracy, in the corner of the store taking down the holiday promotion material. "Hi Tracy. What's going on with the line of the people at the customer service desk?"

"Oh hi Reese. You caught me hiding out taking down this holiday promotion. That line has been going on for the past two days. I just couldn't take the complaints anymore so I begged Amy to take over for me."

"For two days? I have never heard of that! What is everyone complaining about?"

"Well you know Bellingham is a small town and once one person has a problem they tell everyone else; and the next thing you know they all have the problem. It seems the blouses that we ran on special throughout the holidays start to fall apart after one wearing. The sleeves are pulling apart at the shoulder and the buttons fly off when the least amount of pressure is put on them."

"Did you notice this before Christmas?" I asked this question because I had not heard any mention of this problem back in the corporate office.

"Well you know we were so busy before the holidays and most people were not trying on the clothes they were just buying the items quickly to take advantage of the low prices and finish up their shopping. Our problem is that we have such a narrow window during which customers can make their returns and they are all coming in now so that they can get their money back rather than getting a new item. They only have two weeks after Christmas to get their money back and they do not want any to exchange the blouses for other clothes. I'm worried that they have lost trust in us."

I thanked Tracy for the information and then with Carey on my tail, I went looking for Michael, the store manager who took my place. Michael is unusual in that he is a male manager with a staff of primarily young college females. I hired him when I worked in the Bellingham store because he really knew how to talk to the female customers. He had a way of helping them choose clothes that worked best for them so that they would always come back to the store.

I saw Michael talking to two customers who were standing in the returns line. I waited for him to finish his conversation and then went over to catch up.

"Oh Reese, just the person I wanted to see." Michael looked at me like I was his potential savior. "You have to get the corporate office to pay attention to me when I tell them that we have a crisis on our hands."

"What is going on? I've never see you this stressed about something."

"It's these cheaply made blouses. Ever since we started selling them, people started buying them like mad, but they have been falling apart after the first wearing. I tried telling my supervisor about it but he was so focused on us making our sales quota that he really did not do anything about it. Now look at the mess I have to deal with. Not only are my sales down but I am giving out more cash living up to our money back guarantee than I am taking in!"

"I have not heard anything about this problem. Do you think it is just here in Bellingham or are other store managers having the same problem?"

"I haven't had time to talk to anyone else but we have a managers meeting next week to talk about what worked and did not work for the holidays, and this will definitely be at the top of my list."

After this depressing conversation I decided I needed to get out of the store before I betrayed my promise to Carey to not get involved in the operation of the store. "I promise that when I get back to the office on Monday I will find out what's going on. I will get back to you hopefully before your managers meeting."

With that as my parting, and I am sure not so comforting words Carey and I left the store to continue our girl's weekend.

I just couldn't get the image of that line of customers standing at the return desk out of my mind.

Carey sensed that I was preoccupied. "You know just because you work at the corporate office you are not responsible for everything that goes on at Darcy's."

"I know, but I feel that the team here in Bellingham trusts me and I have to at least look into this so that I don't let them down. When I go back to work on Monday, my first step will be to talk to Christine and see if she knows anything about this problem."

After that experience, we decided to treat ourselves to a nice dinner at Anthony's. It was the place we used to go for special occasions and I felt like I needed it. We drove in silence. I was thinking about what Dan had said about work-life balance. And about Dan. Yoga classes had been canceled over Christmas and New Year's, so I hadn't seen him lately.

"Reese, stop thinking about work," Carey said. "I thought you were ready to let it go until Monday and we didn't come up here to think about work!"

I wanted to get her off the subject. But I knew that if I told her about Dan, she and Jack would have me inviting him to dinner with them! On the other hand, she's my best friend and I can't lie to her.

"Carey, I met a guy in yoga. He's—"

"Reese," Carey shrieked, "why didn't you tell me? When? Where? How? What's his name?"

I told her story, such as it was. "His name is Dan and he has a million things going on in his life, so don't get any ideas!"

Carey just laughed. "Then stop blushing, Reese. I know you way too well." While he's not Jack, Dan is the first guy who's turned my head in a long time.

On Sunday night, Jack made dinner. Clearly Jack and Carey have no secrets because over a beer, he toasted to "Reese and Dan." I looked at the two of them and just started laughing.

Chapter 9

I put away tomorrow's dinner and checked my email. My mom had written and I sent her a quick email back so she'd have it when she woke up in the morning. I was surprisingly calm and had a great night's rest.

I got to the office early so I could talk to Jason and get his advice on how to approach the mess that I'd seen in Bellingham. I learned my first week that there are politics and protocol on this team, not to mention strong personalities. I wanted to use this as an opportunity to bond with Christine and perhaps brainstorm solutions we could share together with Sandy, but I wasn't sure she'd be receptive and instead run with it herself. Christine's office door was shut but I could hear her on the phone. Sandy's office was dark. I caught Jason as I walked up the stairs.

"Jason, I think we have a big problem on our hands. I was in Bellingham over the weekend and stopped in at Darcy's to wish my old team a Happy New Year. I thought they were happy to see me, but really they were relieved because they thought I'd come there to help. The return lines were long and ugly, and the store was giving cash refunds to everyone instead of making exchanges!"

He seemed to be distracted, or maybe he was just tired; but I wasn't sure he really understood that what I saw was probably the tip of the iceberg. "Reese, it's probably just a Bellingham thing and I wouldn't get too concerned yet. Remember, you are partial to them." Before I could respond, he said, "I haven't heard a peep about returns, so I'd let it go if I were you."

It was clear he'd be no help, so I bit the bullet and knocked on Christine's door. She looked up and said "Hello," but no more. I shut the door and sat across from her.

"Christine, I think we have a problem." She looked at me intently, and I told her the story in great detail.

She waited until I was finished and simply said, "Reese, you described this as 'typical Bellingham,' so I'm thinking maybe it's just that. You said that the managers were going to have a meeting and I think we should wait until we hear from them so we don't look like alarmists. We've never had quality issues and it could just be a bad lot that went to Bellingham."

I shook my head. "Christine, I told Michael I'd look into it and have something for him to share at the managers meeting. When I managed that store, I always wanted to hear what was going on rather than be surprised later. I think we should tell Sandy. I was hoping that you and I could figure out how to determine if this is widespread so that we could come with something more than complaints."

"Reese, this isn't the store and here, we don't stir up trouble. If you want to go to Sandy, you're on your own. Good luck." And with that, Christine went back to whatever she was reading at her desk.

I was totally being dismissed yet again. I walked back to my cubicle to figure out my next step. The lights were still out in Sandy's office. This was unusual since Sandy was usually one of the first in to the office in the morning. As I sat at my desk, Jason raised his head over the cubicle and said that we had been summoned to a department meeting in the next hour.

"How did you know about the meeting if Sandy still is not in" I asked.

"Sarah came by while you were in with Christine. It seems that Sandy has been called out of the office for personal reasons so Sarah has been put in charge of the department in her absence."

"Sarah? She never says anything and looks like she is afraid of her own shadow. In the meeting with Bill and Clark regarding the tinsel fiasco she looked like she was trying to disappear into the corner of the room."

"She has the most seniority. Remember, she headed up the merchandising department back when Clark started the company and there were only three locations. Slowly but surely she has been bypassed in terms of responsibility, but when Sandy is out she is still the go-to person." Jason seemed to have the pecking order figured out pretty well for only being in the company for one year.

An hour later, we all gathered in the conference room that was nearest to the buying department. Sarah came in last, nervously carrying her notebook and her constant companion, her cell phone. I swear if she was ever separated from her phone, I think she would have a meltdown on the spot. But finally she put it down. "Thanks, everyone, for adjusting your schedules to come to this last-minute meeting. "

"I hope this meeting is important. I have had to postpone an update with the merchandising agent regarding the spring line to make this time work." As always Christine wanted everyone to know how busy and important she is.

Sarah looked at Christine as if she would like to crawl into a hole and totally avoid any potential conflict with the prima donna. "Christine, this meeting was not my idea. Bill will be here in the next fifteen minutes to discuss some current issues that are going on in the stores. He is bringing George from the finance department, too."

"Why do they want to talk to us?" Jason's tone was peevish. "They usually come to us with what they want done but they never come to discuss anything with us."

"Jason your guess is as good as mine, so let's just see what happens. Meanwhile, I hope everyone's holidays were happy and relaxing."

At that moment, Bill swept into the room with George on his heels. I had never met George before, but like everyone else in the company, I knew his name. He had the reputation of being the numbers nerd who was always acting like the sky was falling. If you believed everything he said, you'd think that we would be filing for bankruptcy on a regular basis. True to the image of a finance nerd, he had thick wire-rimmed glasses and believe it or not, he had a pocket protector in his upper pocket. I did not think they even made those anymore.

"Good morning, everyone. I hope you enjoyed your holidays. Thank you, Sarah, for getting your group together on such short notice for me." Bill was known for getting right to the point in his meetings. I remembered this from his visits to me in Bellingham. "I brought George with me to this meeting to talk about a potential problem we have in the stores. As you know, Sandy has been called out of the office and Clark is also out of the office, so this will be the team that needs to solve this issue."

"Of course, Bill, we will do whatever you need. But what is the issue?" Christine asked. All of sudden she had a pen in hand and was poised to write down whatever came out of Bill's mouth.

"Sorry, Christine, I thought that Sarah had already briefed you. We discovered that we have incurred above-average cash returns for holiday. George brought the numbers to me first thing this morning and I am concerned that something must be going on. George, will you please brief the team on what is happening?"

"Sure. As you all know, we monitor the cash returns very closely. We usually have a spike after the holidays. However, this year our cash returns are up two hundred percent from previous levels."

"But weren't our sales up higher than usual? Couldn't that have resulted in the increase in the percentage of returns?" Jason has always prided himself in being able to stand up to finance when it comes to data.

"There should not be any correlation between sales and cash returns if our quality remains consistent," Bill said. "Please listen to George so that we can figure out what is going on."

"Yes, our sales are up and ahead of forecast," George said. "This primarily happened in the last thirty days of the holiday period. It appears that the clothing that was focused on during the month of December was the reason for the increase."

Christine interrupted. "Thank you for reporting that, George. As you know, that promotion was entirely my doing."

"Even so, Christine, it seems from our early reports from the field that the cash returns are focused on this promotion," George said.

"Bill, you know that the stores are notoriously bad at documenting why they are giving out a cash return. I can't believe that you can say that the cash-return problem is all due to this promotion." A whine crept into Christine's voice.

I was having a hard time keeping my mouth shut. I so wanted to tell everyone about my experience in the Bellingham store. But I did not want a repeat of my past conflicts with Christine, so I decided that silence was golden.

"Bill and George, I have been telling you both ever since the company started that we should not have cash returns,"

Sarah cut in. "Especially in these economic times, we could be a victim to customers trying to get some extra money from their holiday presents."

"Sarah, that is why I am asking this team to figure out what is going on," Bill said. "I will leave it to your leadership to get me an answer by the end of the week. Let me know if you need any assistance."

One thing that I learned in the short time that I had been in the corporate office was that you did not want to ask Bill for assistance. That was seen as admitting that you could not do your job.

With those not-very-reassuring words, Bill and George left the room. Sarah looked around like a frightened puppy. "Well, I have to think about this so let's get back together at the end of the day and see if we can strategize as to what to do next."

"Good," Christine said. "I have more important things to do than to solve poor store-execution issues regarding the documentation of cash returns." She picked up her notepad and left. Sarah followed.

Jason and I were left in the conference room. "Jason," I said, "what is the long history between Sarah and Bill regarding cash returns?"

Jason looked at me like he had to educate some poor naïve child. "Reese, you know that Sarah was in charge of merchandising back when the company first started. In reality she just had the title and Clark and Bill made all of the decisions. As the company began to rapidly take off, it became apparent that Sarah would not be able to keep up. She was never able to be innovative with new ideas and was very nervous about any type of change. At the time, the clothing stores never gave cash returns. Clark wanted to prove that Darcy's would stand behind its product, so he mandated that we do what others would not, and that was to give a money-back guarantee.

"Sarah, who as you know is neither visionary nor a risk-taker, freaked out. I think her strong reaction to this policy was the reason that Clark and Bill began to recruit for a new leader for this department."

"Wow," I said. "I never knew all of that history. I remember that it was a big deal when we said that we would give the customers their money back, but frankly since the window for a cash return was so narrow when I was in the stores, we very rarely needed to live up to this promise. But based on what I saw in Bellingham, I am afraid we are focusing on the wrong thing."

"What do you mean?" Jason said, but his eyes were fixed on his phone.

"Well, we could have endless debates regarding the cash-return policy and potential execution issues without looking at the quality issues that are potentially causing this ruckus."

Jason frowned. "My only advice to you before you start down that rabbit hole is that you have real data to back up your claims. Remember this was Queen Christine's project and she will not want anyone, especially you, to say that there was a problem with quality."

With those highly reassuring words, Jason left the room. I barely had time to gather up my notepad before the room was already overrun with next group that was waiting to take over the space.

I walked back to my cube thinking about Jason's advice. I wasn't really sure what would stand up to an interrogation by Christine. So I decided to check with the people who really knew what was going on—the store managers.

I pulled out my list of store managers and began to track down the ones I knew from corporate training classes. I narrowed the list to ten managers based in different parts of the country, and began dialing the selected managers on the East Coast so that I could catch them before they left for the day.

"Hi, Justine," I said to the first name on my list, "this is Reese from the corporate office. I used to be the manager from the Bellingham store and we attended the profit-maker class together."

"Oh, sure, Reese. I remember you. What can I do for you?"

I was relieved to have her attention. Justine was the manager of a high-volume store in Albany, New York. She had been a manager for at least five years and in all my contact with her, she never seemed to overreact.

"I was just checking on the results of your sales from holiday. What seemed to sell well and what needs to be improved?" I did not want Christine to say that I planted the idea that there was a quality problem.

"Reese, since you are now working at the corporate office, I am really glad you called," Justine said. "I have not been able to get anyone's attention about the problems we have had with the blouses that were featured for the holiday promotion."

"Oh really. What is the problem?" I grabbed my notepad.

"The blouses are falling apart. My regular customers are so frustrated that they are asking for their money back rather than taking a chance on other items that could have the same quality issue. We did not notice this before Christmas because, frankly, most people were just scooping up the sale items and not bothering to try on any of the clothes. But ever since New Year's we have been flooded with returns. I am sure that the fact that this has been picked up by the local Albany blog has escalated the communication of the problem."

"The Albany blog?" I asked. "How does that work?"

"Oh, you know in these towns the days of waiting until the morning paper comes out to spread news is past history. Now the local blog publishes items twenty-four-seven and everyone uses it to share the latest news in the community. Someone came out and said 'Let's see if Darcy's really will stand by its money-back guarantee now that we have obviously got a problem with our clothes.' I think some of our competitors have used it as a challenge to show that we will not live up to our word."

"I don't remember us having this problem before. Do you?"

"No, I don't remember this problem either. But we have grown so fast recently and we have never tried to promote this type of clothing at this low of a price point during the holiday time period."

"I suppose that's true," I said. "Thanks for taking the time, Justine, and I will get back to you when I find out what is going on."

Almost every call I made that afternoon was a repeat of my conversation with Justine. In small towns where our stores were located, the community blog was the primary vehicle for information. And bad news traveled quickly.

I had been on the phone nonstop for three hours when Jason tapped me on the shoulder. I looked up and he tapped his watch. I hung up with the store manager from Fort Smith, Arkansas to whom I was talking. "You have been at this nonstop all afternoon. How are you planning on sharing this information with the rest of us? Remember we are getting back together in the next fifteen minutes."

I had completely lost track of time. "Thanks, Jason. I just wanted to have some facts before we went back into the meeting. The last thing I wanted was to go to a meeting just to decide that we needed to have another meeting. That run-around in the short time I have been here is driving me crazy."

"Okay, well, it is show time," he said. "So let's go see how they react to your fact-finding mission."

We walked back into the meeting room. This time only Christine and Sarah were there, as Sarah had not included Bill and George. "Team," Sarah began, "I think we need to take this time to make the recommendation to abolish the cash-return policy." After what Jason told me, I saw that once Sarah has a point she wants to prove she does not give up. "I have been telling Clark and Bill for years that no one else does this, and I think it is too risky for us to lead the charge. This episode is just what we need to prove my point."

Jason looked at me and gave me a not-so-subtle sign that I should speak up. "Sarah," I began, "I hear what you are saying about the return policy. However I have been making some phone calls today."

Christine broke in. "What! You have been making calls without us planning what you should say? You are new here and if you say the wrong thing, it will be bad for all of us."

"Christine, if you would give me a chance I will tell you what I did. I merely called managers that I already knew to ask them how their holidays were."

Sarah spoke up. "Christine is right, Reese. You should not call the stores unless we all agree on what is going to be said. But if you only called managers that you knew to talk about the holidays, it should be okay."

"Yes, that is all that I did."

"Well, what did they say?" Christine demanded.

"Well it seems that all of them are having problems with the blouses that were promoted over the holidays. In addition, in these small towns, communication has been taken over by the local blogs or other internet sources."

"I don't see what that has to do with anything." Sarah, as a working mother of two, does not spend any time on social media.

"Sarah, this means that in the past, it could take a couple of days for information to travel throughout these small towns—whereas today, that happens in couple of hours."

Jason was trying to be patient as he explained. I'd printed out a few of the blog posts and handed them out as Jason talked.

"Oh I guess I never thought about that." Sarah said quietly, reading one or two posts. "But what does this have to do with our problem?"

I continued on. "Well, it seems that our competitors have jumped on the fact that we have a quality issue, and they want to see if we will honor our money-back guarantee. They are making sure that everyone in the town knows what is going on, as if they're challenging us." The room fell silent. I really wished that Sandy was back to tell us what to do next.

Sarah looked as if she wished anyone but her to be in charge. "Well, since you have started this research, Reese, I think you need to summarize it so that we can take it to the executive committee, who can decide what the next step should be. Sorry to be so abrupt but since it is close to five o'clock, I need to go and pick up my children." With those less-than-motivating words, Sarah flew out of the room.

"Reese, are you sure about the quality issues?" Christine said. "I will be interested in seeing your detailed write-up since

I think you may have misinterpreted what the managers were saying. This could just be some sort of social-media push to make us give up on our money-back return policy."

Since this conversation was not going anywhere, we left the room, and Jason and I continued the discussion at our desks. "Reese, take a deep breath and go home. You are not going to win this battle tonight. I will help you with your write-up tomorrow."

Chapter 10

January in Seattle is depressing after the festiveness of the holidays. The streets were eerily empty and very quiet. Bellingham never felt that much different after the holidays, so I was at a loss for how to process my frustration with Sarah and Christine. I decided to walk home and get lost in my thoughts, hoping for the answers to come.

As I walked toward the waterfront, I saw a group of runners as I came down the back of Harbor Steps. At least there were a few people breathing life into the city. I wondered how it was that they could make time for this, how they got out of work early enough to run, and how they could take their minds off work.

I found myself walking at a pretty fast clip because I was frustrated with everything, especially the fact that no one other than me seemed to really see the issue on the horizon. Did no one care? I just didn't get it.

Clearly I wasn't paying attention to my surroundings. I stepped off the curb to cross the street, heard tires screech and then a loud horn honking. I was so distracted that I had walked through a red light with rush-hour traffic starting to pour through the intersection. I froze in my tracks, which just made it worse, then I ran onto the sidewalk and continued home. My heart was beating a mile a minute. *It's a sign, Reese.* The words popped into my head. I was too focused on work and was missing the real world.

I calmed down as I walked further along, past the yoga studio. I knew there were classes every night, but I was afraid the other classes were too challenging and that I'd look like a fool if I tried to take one. I peeked inside the window and to my surprise, saw Dan front and center in the class. I remember what he'd said about practicing yoga, which made me feel stupid for not trying harder.

I didn't want him to see me, so I kept walking toward home, but my thoughts were of our conversation weeks before. I started to remember what he said about finding balance and realized I wasn't very good at it. Things had to change. I just didn't know if I actually could.

I got home and called Carey to see if she'd meet me for a walk or slow run, but she and Jack were on their way to meet some friends for a quick dinner. She asked if I'd join them, but I was determined to do something active while I was motivated. I settled for a detour to my loft and took the stairs instead of the elevator. And I recommitted to Wednesday yoga with the intent of adding two more classes a week.

I turned on the television to listen to the news and went online to check the yoga studio class schedule. There was a later class tonight, but I was warm and ready to settle in after my "long walk." There was a class on Tuesday – some form of yoga I hadn't tried before – but I was on a mission and needed to take advantage of it.

Tuesday morning came all too quickly. As I got to my desk, I said, "Jason, let's get going" to the general direction of his cube. He rolled out his chair.

"Reese, let's get this report done so we can put this back into Sarah's hands," he said. "She has to be the one to deliver the recommendation to Bill and George because they gave her the lead. And you don't want to be the one in the center of this firestorm anyway. Let's go."

We worked furiously for nearly two hours, but when we were done, we were really pleased with the report. I handed it to Sarah and turned to walk away.

"Reese, what is this? I thought we agreed that this was a refund-policy issue that is being blown out of proportion by the internet."

"Sarah, I never agreed with that. We need to look at the customers' reason for returning the same item in multiple stores. And if we pull back on the refund policy now, we will lose all credibility with our customers. This is about our reputation, not just the numbers."

I could tell that Sarah had no idea what I was talking about. The business classes at Western taught us about reputation as one measurement of a company's success, so I was sensitive to it. Profit was important but not the only thing that mattered.

"Sarah, what is our next step? What do you plan to do?"

She looked through me. "I'm going to recommend that we stop the bleeding and only offer store credit from here on out. We can say that too much time has passed since Christmas."

"Sarah, you were asked to lead this and you are free to make that recommendation, but I can't support it." With that I walked away, with Sarah right on my heels.

"Reese, so you're going to undermine me in front of my peers?"

"Sarah, you don't have to have me in the room when you meet with Bill and George."

"But if you're not there, they'll ask why." I could tell she wasn't getting this at all.

"You don't have to answer for me, Sarah. Once you have your meeting and make your recommendation, I'll send my findings to Bill and George, and let them decide what to do with them. This way, it's not your issue, okay?"

I could tell she was relieved. I was worried that my absence would give Christine the opportunity to slam me in front of the execs, so I decided I would tell her what I planned to do.

In her office, I went through my data while she sat, speechless. I knew it was risky because she owned this promotion, but I felt the truth had to come out. "Christine, you couldn't have known there would be quality issues and it's not your fault. But I think we have a problem and if we cover it up, then we become part of it." I felt like my mother now, as if this was a parent-child teaching moment, but I hoped Christine wouldn't see it that way and get offended.

"Reese, I know you're trying to do the right thing here, but it's only ten stores out of one thousand. I think we should be extra sure this is a problem before we bring it up. If you can spend the day calling more stores and we can validate this with fifty, I'll take the report to Clark myself."

I was a little surprised and not thrilled that I had forty calls to make, but I was glad to see her finally take an interest in this issue. I agreed with her plan.

By five p.m., I felt like a robot and not a person, but I had validated the story forty more times. I had been adding to the report throughout the day, so I put the final touches on it and slid it under Christine's door.

The yoga class was not as full as the others and I didn't recognize the instructor or any of the other students. I found a place in the back so I could follow others in the class. As I was resting in child's pose, there was a tap on my shoulder. There stood Dan.

"It's a surprise to see you on Tuesday night. What got into you?" he said with a chuckle.

I was sure I was blushing because I was suddenly warm with embarrassment, but I wrote it off to the heat in the room. "It's been far too long since my last class and I need to put more focus on to things other than work."

"Hmmm, that sounds familiar..." he said, and walked away to claim a spot up front.

The class was hard and different than the Wednesday class, but I was glad I was there. Dan and I walked out together and he asked if I wanted to stop for a quick bite. Of course I did. I wanted to introduce him to Carmine's because I thought he'd like it, but I could just picture Carmine's face if I brought a guy with me. He'd either embarrass me, embarrass Dan or embarrass us both. I suggested a little pho place on the way to my loft.

We compared holiday stories while we waited for our orders to arrive. Dan had spent his holidays with family in and out of town, and had one funny story after the next. I didn't feel nearly as entertaining, but I did tell him in great detail about the girls' weekend I spent with Carey. I purposely avoided the Darcy's story because I didn't want another lecture.

"Why didn't you visit your folks this holiday?" Dan said. "I don't know if I could stand to spend holidays completely away from mine."

I didn't know how to respond because I was sure he'd think I was making excuses. "It was crazy busy at work and I didn't feel I could take time away from work, let alone unpaid vacation time. My parents understood and I promised to visit them as soon as my vacation kicks in," I explained, but he shook his head.

"I understand that, but remember that they won't be around forever. Don't take them for granted." I didn't have a response and after a long silence, he changed the subject back to yoga.

I was relieved to talk about yoga, so we did that until our food came. As we ate, I asked him questions about Seattle and what he loved about it. He told more great stories about things to do and see; it was really fun. It was late and I asked if he'd walk me to my loft.

"I'll walk you to your loft if you'll agree to spend the day with me on Saturday," Dan said. "I'd like to show you some of the more unique things about Seattle."

I was stunned by this proposition but said "okay" before I could think straight. "Where are we going? What are we doing? What should I wear?" I felt like I was in high school and I was acting the part, too.

He just looked at me and smiled as we stood in front of my building. "You'll see. Nothing too dangerous. Jeans, comfortable shoes and bring a warm jacket. Have a good evening and I'll see you back here on Saturday at noon. Oh, and come hungry." With that, he turned and walked away.

I bounded up the stairs and called Carey. I told her everything and she was laughing the entire time. "Stop getting so hyper about this," she said "Go with an open mind and make sure I have his cell number in case you don't show up for work on Monday and they call me trying to find you!"

"That's ridiculous. Of course I'll be at work on Monday. In fact, I'll call you when I get home on Saturday night from this whatever this is."

"You mean 'date,' Reese."

"Whatever." We hung up and I was feeling really good until I remembered the issues at work. When would this come to a head?

Wednesday at work was, surprisingly, a normal day. I saw Sarah, but she didn't tell me anything about next steps. Christine thanked me for the report and said, "Nice job, I'll take it from here." So I went back to my real job and left in time for Wednesday yoga. Dan wasn't there.

The rest of the week flew by with no word from Bill about the quality problems. I spoke with Michael on Friday, who confirmed that the majority of store managers had given cash for returned merchandise and that he understood corporate was "working on it."

I thought it odd that neither Christine nor Sarah brought it up to me again, so I asked Jason what he thought. "Reese, this is the corporate world and things don't always happen in real time. I'm sure people more important than us are figuring it out. Stop worrying and have a nice weekend."

Jason was a good guy who was clearly looking out for me, so I took his advice and went home to make sure I had clean jeans and a decent sweater. I wasn't sure what to think about this "date" with Dan, but I'd find out soon.

Chapter 11

I was downstairs a few minutes before noon after changing my clothes so many times that I couldn't remember what I liked anymore. It was an uncharacteristically sunny day in Seattle in January and I had a little bounce in my step. I could see Dan crossing the street and resisted the urge to walk toward him. He smiled as he greeted me and said, "Let's go!"

"I feel the need to show you Seattle the way it grew up. When you look at the skyline today, you sometimes lose the history of this amazing city."

We walked up First Avenue toward the Pergola, which is this beautiful iron shelter that was built as a cable car stop and marks the true center of Pioneer Square. By its side sits a large totem pole that has been there since 1899.

"This totem pole is said to have been stolen from the Tlingit Indians in Alaska by members of the Chamber of Commerce. They were fined five hundred dollars for the theft but the city was allowed to keep the totem pole. What you see is a reproduction of the original pole, also carved by the Tlingit Indians, after vandals set the original one on fire."

I suddenly felt like the student to his teacher, but I didn't let on. "What do you think it was like here in 1899?" That was the lamest thing I think I've ever said!

"I'm going to show you that shortly," he said as we crossed the street and approached a nearby building. "We are going to take the Underground Tour today. It's amazing and will answer all of your questions."

"Underground Tour? I heard something about that when I was at Western. Some friends came down for a weekend and took the tour, but I didn't ask much about it at the time."

Dan smiled. "I remember the first time I took the tour. I was about twelve and my cousins were visiting from Minneapolis. They wanted to go, so my parents took all of us. I think I've been back at least a half dozen times since then. It never grows old."

He bought our tickets despite my insistence on funding myself. The tour started inside Doc Maynard's Public House, a restored 1890s saloon. After a short introductions, we roamed through subterranean passages beneath the city streets and sidewalks. At certain corners, you could look up through fused glass and see people walking above. I felt transcended as the guide told stories that you don't find in history books!

Dan added his own commentary here and there, but I was determined to ask questions when we were done with the tour. And I was getting hungry!

"Let's walk into downtown. There is this great soup place I want you to try."

As we walked along First, I could see glimpses of the water at each cross street. And after the tour, I kept thinking about the hills, why the city grew up this way and how different life would have been if the Great Fire hadn't been.

"You look totally lost in your thoughts," Dan said.

"I am just imaging how life was in the underground and how smart it was to create higher ground," I said. "The tour was like a secret that Seattle has shared with me and that's pretty cool."

He broke out in a grin and simply said, "I knew you'd get it" as he opened the door to a little café with standing room only.

"Let's order and I'll try to snag two spots at the window bar. The people-watching is pretty great." He paid yet again. The soup was amazing—filling and warming—and when we were done, we continued to north into the heart of downtown.

I was tempted to look at windows displaying women's clothing, but I refrained. We bantered more about the tour and had great laughs speculating about how hard it would have been to actually steal a totem pole. Suddenly, we were at Westlake Center, which housed this old-fashioned carousel during the holidays. We crossed Westlake and the next thing I knew, we boarded a Ducks tour vehicle with official Duck whistles in hand.

"Now you will see another unique part of Seattle, including those that live on the water," Dan said. The Ducks tour uses a vehicle that is also a boat. It's large and open air, much like a tourist bus. Who knew? We were joined by a large group of people who were from Cleveland, which made us both chuckle. "I'm a Seattle native with a large family in Minneapolis," Dan said. "What about you?"

"Born and raised in North Dakota, where my entire family continues to live. The Pacific Northwest seemed to call to me but I was afraid of a big city at the time I went to college and Western was more my style than U-Dub. Maybe that's why we can appreciate the Clevelanders."

"I just hope they ask lots of questions, know how to have fun and can sing."

"Sing? What are we singing?"

"Whatever the driver tells us to!" And then Dan added while laughing, "Just sit back and enjoy the ride before the true fun begins!"

The driver was more of an entertainer and he really knew how to draw all of us out of our shells. We had a blast! The best part was when we went down the boat ramp into Lake Union, took a tour of the houseboats and saw the *Sleepless in Seattle* one. I kept waiting for Jonah to walk out of the house; that's how real it felt.

The next part of the tour gave us the history of the upper city, if you will, in Pioneer Square. "Dan, now I see why we started underground." He just smiled but was silent.

We returned to Westlake Center and Dan asked if I liked martinis. It seemed like such a strange question after this very intense day, but that was Dan—Mr. Eclectic.

"I'm a Cosmo girl, if you must know."

"Yes, I must. Let's go. As we rounded the corner, we walked into the Mayflower Park Hotel. I must confess it was funny in a weird way, walking into a hotel on a first date. I was also relieved when we walked into the hotel bar, Oliver's.

"This is probably on my top three lists of bars in Seattle," Dan said. "The bartenders know how to make cocktails, conversation and take care of their guests. I love to come here and have a beer, and just talk to whomever is at the bar. Other times, I enjoy watching them make a good martini. I thought this would be a great way to round out the day."

I felt a little disappointed that this might be the end of the day, but I didn't say anything.

As if Dan read my mind, he said, "Reese, I had a great day today and I'm meeting some friends for dinner. You are more than welcome to join us if you'd like. They're law-school friends and we've been through the best and worst together. You'd especially enjoy Martin—all the girls do!"

Now I was confused. Our drinks came and we toasted to a great day. I took a big gulp. "Sounds fun," I managed. "I'd love to."

We chatted more about the two tours as we finished our drinks. "I'm meeting them at a little pizza place a few blocks from here, so when you're ready, let's go."

It occurred to me that must have been pretty confident he'd get a "yes" because I didn't think he'd send me home alone in the dark.

We went to a place called Serious Pie and it was indeed very serious pizza. And delicious. We all had a great time and his friends were really fun. Martin was certainly handsome but a little full of himself. We all waved goodbye, and Dan and I walked toward my place.

"Dan that was a great day," I said. "Thank you so much for showing me the real Seattle. Your friends were really fun, too."

It felt like blocks until he said, "I had fun today, too. Thanks for spending the time and agreeing to my antics."

It was suddenly very awkward and neither of us said much more, with my loft in plain sight. "I'm going on a hike early tomorrow, so I'm going to call it a night and get some sleep, Reese. Have a great Sunday and I will see you soon." We hugged goodbye and he was gone.

I admit that when I got out into my place, I literally melted into the couch. It had been a great day, but between the fresh air and all the walking, I was tired. I was also distracted by a burning question: Was that a date?" I figured I'd process it six ways to Sunday with Carey at some point.

The sun was shining when I woke up the next morning, but within a few hours the clouds and rain rolled in. I wondered if Dan was out there hiking in the cold and suddenly realized I didn't really have a way to get a hold of him. I decided to put the whole thing out of my mind. And thoughts of work started to creep into my brain.

I looked online and saw there was a yoga class in an hour, so I decided to go. It was my way of getting ahead of my commitment to go three times a week – yay, me.

Chapter 12

A light on in Sandy's office as I walked into work Monday morning. I was relieved that she was back. Perhaps now I would know what was really going on.

No sooner had I sat at my cube than I felt Sandy's presence over my shoulder. "Reese will you please come to my office and bring me up to speed on what has been happening while I was away." She turned and walked back to her office. I grabbed my notes and followed her.

"I understand that we have had an issue over the holiday with the return policy," Sandy began.

"Sandy, I don't think that is really the issue; the issue is that the blouses that we had on promotion are falling apart after one wearing."

Sandy reached for a report on her desk. "This is the report that was given to the executive team. It is a highly detailed account of the failure of the stores to properly adhere and document details regarding cash returns. The assumption in this report is that we had fraud occurring in the stores to give out cash after the holidays."

"That is not the report that I prepared for Christine and Sarah. If my name is attached to that report that is not right."

"I do not have time to get into a 'he said she said' debate. I just want to know what is going on."

Before I had a chance to tell Sandy the rest of the story Clark came charging into Sandy's office. "Sandy it seems that while I was out last week everyone started re-debating my cash-return policy. Now this is a topic on the Jim Cramer's news show and I have to answer to him about it. What the hell is going on?"

"Clark, calm down!" Sandy said. "Reese and I were just discussing this very topic. Let me finish my discussion with her and I will come to your office and help you handle your response to Cramer."

"No, I will not be dismissed when my company is under attack. This is the worst thing that's ever happened to the company. I will stay and hear what Reese has to say."

I have never been so scared in my life. Seeing Clark swearing and being red in the face about a topic that I have knowledge about is not what I would wish on my worst enemy, not even Christine!

"By the way, where are Christine and Sarah?" Clark said.

"Christine has left to go overseas to handle the orders for the spring merchandising plans and Sarah has taken a personal day off." Sandy seemed to be up to date on what everyone was scheduled to do even though she had been out of pocket.

"Okay, Reese, please tell us what is going on," Clark said impatiently.

With that as my lead in I gave both of them a recap of my trip to Bellingham and the subsequent follow up calls to the fifty stores.

"In spite of this data, it seems that the entire group was more focused on the execution of the return policy rather than the true cause of the returns." I am sure that my frustration at both Sarah and Christine was coming through. I should have known that the lack of follow-up last week after Christine had said she delivered my report was an indication that she had not been truthful. When will I ever stop trusting people and learn to follow up on these things on my own?

"Sandy, you and I are going to fly to Vietnam immediately to see what is going on. Clear your schedule for a departure tomorrow."

"Clark, whatever you want. I think that Reese should go with us."

"That is fine. Just make it happen."

I was now in a state of shock. I had a passport for trips to Canada, but I had never flown overseas much less flown on the corporate jet. Clark spun and flew out of Sandy's office.

"Now you see why Clark is the CEO," Sandy said. "He makes things happen and does not tolerate anything going wrong when it comes to quality in his stores."

"How can we possibly be ready to go to Vietnam tomorrow?" I said.

"We can't but we will. Let me coordinate with Clark's administrative assistant and I will find out if this trip really is possible in this time frame. You need to find out the name of

113

the agent who is responsible for coordinating all of the overseas manufacturing and tell him about our plans. Don't give him too much information because I do not want him to have time to cover up any problems we may see."

By the time I went back to my desk, still in a state of shock, Jason had arrived. "Hi, Reese. How was your weekend?"

Jason was clueless as to the 'hailstorm' I had just been through. When I did not immediately answer he looked at my face and said 'What just happened?"

"Clark had a meltdown in Sandy's office over the holiday return drama and immediately wants Sandy, and unfortunately me, to go with him to Vietnam to see what is going on."

"Oh, you have now witnessed Clark on a raving rampage," Jason said. "Sandy usually is the only one that can calm him down and create some sense of reason when he goes off like this."

"Easy for you to say but I have never traveled overseas and I have no idea how the manufacturing process works over there." Jason could see that I was completely over my head.

"Go meet with Harry in the distribution department. He can give you a fast primer and also can give you the names of our contacts in Vietnam." Jason gave me Harry's contact info.

Less than an hour later, I found myself sitting in front of Harry Silverstein. He was situated in an office on the fourth floor in the far corner. I don't think anyone had ever visited him in his office before, as it was littered with paper piles everywhere. His office would be a great candidate for the TV show *Hoarders*. His rumpled shirt and wrinkled tie seemed appropriate. I don't think he had ever thrown out a single sheet of paper and the computer only seemed to be an instrument to generate more paper.

"I don't usually meet with people here but you seemed so desperate that I made an exception," he said. "Explain to me what is going on." As disorganized as his office seemed to be Harry seemed very calm and on top of his business.

"Well, it seems we have a quality problem with the clothing we sold over holidays and Clark wants to make an immediate trip to Vietnam."

He seemed to get it. "I told Christine that what she was doing with this promotion was risky," Harry said.

"What do you mean?"

"Christine wanted to change our agent for sourcing in Vietnam," Harry explained. "She ran this change through without letting any of us vet this guy. She was all excited about the savings that she knew he could get for us so she went over my head and signed this guy on."

"Who is this guy?" This was the name I was supposed to get.

"He is supposedly a friend of Clark's, and Christine met with him based on Clark's recommendation. You know when Clark recommends someone, you need to at least meet with them."

I had heard of the "friend of Clark" title but I did not think Christine would risk the quality of the clothes just to please upper management. Will I ever stop being surprised at what goes on in this building?

"His name is Juan Gomez. He and Clark supposedly went to school together. He is a true salesman. When I met with him with Christine I was not happy with the slick answers that he gave to Christine. She was under pressure to make the promotion for holiday work so she probably did not want to believe that 'if it seems to be too good to be true that may be the case'. I told her that I could not support this guy and she went over my head to my vice president to make it happen. I think Sandy was aware of all of this."

It seemed that in some perverse way that Harry was happy to be delivering this bad news to me. "Well, it looks like I will need to meet this gentleman," I said. "Thanks for the info and I will keep you up to date with what happens."

"Thanks. We are in process of making an even larger order for the spring promotion. We only have a short window of time to make any changes if we expect to have product in the stores on time for the change in season."

I left Harry's office totally depressed. I walked up the stairs to my desk staring at my feet the entire time. What had I gotten into with my move to Seattle?

Chapter 13

Mom and Dad, I am writing you a quick e-mail from hot, muggy but beautiful Vietnam. Who would have ever thought that I would be visiting this country after hearing all of your stories Dad about the war? By the way over here they call it the American War and they are quite proud of the results. We arrived yesterday and today I have been on my own to recover from jet lag. I promise to take lots of pictures and I will give you all of the details regarding the flight on the corporate jet once I return.

After letting my parents know that I was alive, I decided to explore the area. Clark, Sandy and I had flown seventeen hours to Ho Chi Minh City (I had always known it as Saigon), obtained our visas, and continued on for another hour to central Vietnam and the city of Danang. By this point I was totally comatose so after taking a taxi to our final destination in Hoi An, I literally crashed in my hotel room.

When I regained consciousness, I tried calling Sandy but could not connect with her. I decided to explore the area on my own. Hoi An is a beautiful village. Everyone rides bicycles and street vendors were calling to me to take a cycle trip. This is a basket on two wheels that is pulled by a man riding a bicycle. Maybe later.

The little village wraps around the Thu Bon River, which led to the Pacific Ocean. This entire area is focused on tourists and clothing manufacture. The tourists come from all over and have custom-made suits made for them in no more than two days. No wonder we were able to get our holiday-promotion clothes so cheaply.

After wandering around for a couple of hours I decided I had better return to the hotel and join up with Sandy. But the streets are tiny and curvy and of course I got lost. So my short walk back took me at least an hour.

I entered into the old but quaint hotel and, sure enough, there was Sandy waiting in the lobby. "Reese, we were about ready to call the police to find you. What have you been doing?"

I knew my explanation sounded lame.

"We need to meet with Juan Gomez in thirty minutes. Please change and meet us in the lobby bar." Sandy was definitely taking a very strict motherly tone with me. I felt like I was about five years old.

After running up to my room, and putting on fresh clothes and tying my unruly hair into a bun—hopefully to give me a more adult appearance)—I walked into the lobby bar where Sandy, Clark and this beautiful gentleman were having drinks.

Clark waved me over. "Oh Reese, I am glad that you were able to join us. Sandy was not sure if you had fully recovered from the flight over. Let me introduce you to Juan Gomez. Juan and I have known each other for years."

To call Juan beautiful is an understatement. He is tall, fit, and has dark brown eyes that seem to look only at you. I have never seen someone with such a great smile and such perfect teeth. "Reese it is a pleasure to meet you. I am so glad that you will be able to join us tonight for dinner. I think that Christine is also arriving today from Hanoi, so if the three of you do not mind, I have also invited her to join us."

"Of course we do not mind. I was wondering where Christine was," Clark said graciously. We ordered drinks.

"Now Juan, tell me what you have been up to. I have not seen you for at least five years." The two began reminiscing about their early years together. I stopped listening after hearing Clark say he had not spoken to Juan for at least five years. Somehow this "friend of Clark's" was not quite the close compadre that Harry had led me to believe.

Just when we had finished our drinks and began discussing what we wanted for dinner, Christine entered the bar. As usual, she looked totally put together with her blonde hair perfectly styled and a sleeveless red designer dress that could easily have been a St. Laurent. How much money must she make to buy such fancy things? You would never have known that she had just flown in from Hanoi.

"Hi everyone, Clark, Sandy. Reese, it is a surprise to see you here. Juan told me you were coming and I couldn't believe it, but I am delighted to show you what we have planned for the spring merchandise selection."

"Christine, this trip was my idea," Clark said. "I owe it to the company that before we make the investment as large as you are planning for spring that I verify the quality and competency of the manufacturing facility."

"Of course, Clark. I am really happy to have you here so that Juan can show you all the precautions we have taken to make sure that the clothes meet your standards as well as deliver on the targeted price point." Christine seemed to speak of Juan with a sense of kindness I'd not heard before. And there was this enamored look in her eyes as she spoke.

"That's enough shop talk. "Juan interrupted. "I think that it is important for all of us to have a delightful dinner and then we can talk shop tomorrow. As you may know, Hoi An is as famous for its food as it is for custom clothing. Many tourists come here just to participate in the cooking schools. Every restaurant offers these classes to show off their expertise. Even though the Vietnamese were not happy to be occupied by the French, they definitely incorporated the high standards of French cooking in their cuisine. I suggest that we go to one my favorite sites by the river, the Cargo Club."

Moments later, we were settled on the terrace of the Cargo Club. I looked out at the activity on the river and watched the fishermen returning with their catch.

"This is beautiful," I said. Not at all what I imagined after hearing all about the war from my Dad and watching *Platoon*.

"This area really was not touched by the conflict. As you noticed when you flew into Danang, we are right by China Beach. This was the area that the soldiers could have some type of retreat from the battles in the jungles." Juan was trying to graciously educate me about a period of history to which I had paid little attention.

Dinner was truly amazing and I was proud of myself for trying things I'd never heard of. Carmine would definitely be proud that his "spaghetti and red sauce girl" had stepped out—he's always trying to get me to try something different. The alcohol was flowing, but I chose to keep it at a minimum because I didn't want to get another stern look from Sandy.

When we arrived back at the hotel, both Sandy and Clark claimed exhaustion and moved toward the elevators. "Juan, thank you for a lovely evening. It was great to see you again after all this time." Clark vigorously shook Juan's hand.

The doors to the elevator closed and Christine perked up, facing Juan. "Now that those two are on their own, I think we should share some sticky rice wine."

I clearly had a look of confusion on my face, but Christine quickly said, "Reese, sticky rice wine is a local beverage—a shot—is customarily shared by friends. In fact, they often share shot glasses, but I think we'll each have our own shot."

"Reese, you're lucky to be here with Clark, Sandy and Christine, and I think Christine is right—let's finish off the night with one more traditional Vietnamese custom." With that, Juan led us to the bar.

"Christine, I always enjoy seeing you. Reese, it's been wonderful to meet you," Juan said as we clicked our glasses.

The reddish brown liquid in my glass tasted sweet, smooth and warm as it trickled down my throat. I was partway through my shot when I realized this was to be drunk like tequila—that is, quickly. Christine and Juan's glasses were already empty and Juan had signaled for three more. I finished my first and was pleased to feel very little effect from the alcohol. The second went down easily.

The conversation between the three of us was stilted and soon morphed into me watching Christine and Juan debate something about Vietnamese history that I didn't quite understand. As the debate continued, I could see the romantic intensity between them grow, and it was making me uncomfortable. As I stood to excuse myself, Juan quickly rose and said, "Good night, ladies. I'll leave you two to talk about the factory visit tomorrow."

"Reese, I hope Sandy and Clark's departure wasn't as weird for you as it was for me," Christine said. "I've gotten used to them meeting behind closed doors, but that was a little abrupt."

I didn't know what she was driving at, so I decided to avoid a discussion. To be honest, watching Christine and Juan was weird; I hadn't thought anything of Sandy and Clark leaving because of the magnitude of the spring order, especially given the holiday issue we had.

She pressed on. "I suppose they have the ultimate say in the spring order and wanted some private time to discuss it. I just think that could have waited for tomorrow."

"Maybe they were both just tired," I said. Of course, that was met with a near eye roll as Christine finished her glass of water and rose.

"Well, I'm off to sleep. Long day tomorrow. I assume you know where we're meeting?"

"Yes. I was hoping to catch a cab with you, Sandy or Clark."

"Well, I think you should plan to go on your own. Sandy and Clark will likely have an early breakfast, and I have something I want to do on my way." With that, she was gone.

I gathered my jacket and headed for the elevator. I guess Christine caught one quickly because she was nowhere to be found. When I got to my room, I called down for a wakeup call and taxi to the factory. It was going to be a long day and I wanted to be alert and prepared. And I wanted to put aside the suspicions that were put in front of me earlier.

Chapter 14

After a somewhat sleepless night, I decided to have a good breakfast before heading to the factory. Even after an amazing dinner, I was hungry for a big, American breakfast. Carmine would say I was making up for having eaten something "different" the night before; and that brought a smile to my face. This trip was an opportunity for me, but I was looking forward to my own bed.

As I ate breakfast, I kept an eye open for Christine, Sandy or Clark. As I did, I realized I was also thinking about Christine's comments. Was she trying to tell me something or simply protecting me? I wanted to trust her. I could hear my mother saying, "Reese, you have to always find the good in people." My gut just wasn't sure.

I took care of my check and went outside to wait for the taxi. I had the factory address given to me in Seattle tucked away in my wallet so I wouldn't get lost this time. I really needed to make sure I left a more favorable impression on Sandy and Clark.

An old rickety cab pulled up in front of the hotel. "I can take you wherever you want to go very cheap". I was skeptical about whether or not this cab would even make it to the factory, but I did not want to be late. "Fine here is the address."

"Oh madam, I am sure you have the wrong address. No one visits this place."

"What do you mean; isn't this a manufacturing site?"

"Yes, but no one ever goes here from this hotel."

"Just take me there as I have an appointment at 9 a.m."

I arrived 15 minutes early on purpose and waited for the others to arrive. I sat in the cab and did not see any activity around this large building surrounded by a high fence. When the clock hit 9 a.m., our appointed meeting time, I began to wonder if there was a different entrance on the side or back of the building, so I decided to take a walk around. "Please wait right here for me. I need to see if my friends are at the back of the building."

"OK. But if the guards come out I will need to leave you. I don't want to get in trouble."

As I circled the building, I saw a palette of boxes marked "Darcy's," so I knew I was in the right place. But where was everyone? I tried to call both Sandy and Christine on their cell phones, but both went straight to voicemail. On the third try, I left them both a message that I was here and waiting.

Thank goodness for the camera on my phone. I decided I needed to take pictures of the boxes in the yard at the rear of the building. I was lining up my camera to capture the shot through an opening in the fence when I heard the motor of my cab start up. Oh no! I can't get caught here. I ran around the building just in time to see my cab take off with a guard standing in the road watching it depart. Now what was I going to do.

I had no choice. I needed to talk to the guard and see if I could get another ride back to the hotel. He was only five feet tall and just about as wide as he was tall. I approached him from the rear and said "Excuse me."

He was obviously startled as he turned around, but oh my, he had a gun in his hand. "Sir, I am supposed to meet my friends here and you just chased off my ride back to the hotel"

He just grunted at me and obviously did not speak English. "You leave. No one is here"

"How can I leave when you chased off my ride?"

"You go now. Leave"

He was waving that gun around wildly so I decided further conversation was not going to work.

I took off down the road back towards town. After getting out of sight of the plant I took off my shoes and started walking barefoot. I had no idea what I was going to do. It was hot, muggy, and my feet were killing me. *I wondered if he would have fired the gun had I not left.*

After walking for what seemed like days, even though it was only a couple of hours, I came to the main intersection of the road. There was a crowd of people standing by the road at what looked to be a bus stand. I went up to them "Does anyone here speak English?"

A little girl who was only about eight years old looked at me and said "I do."

"Is this a bus back to the Hoi An?"

She looked up to her mother probably to see if it was okay to talk to this dirty, sweaty woman. Her mother gave her a small nod. "Yes this is the bus. It will be here in 15 minutes."

When the bus came I climbed on with everyone else. The bus was probably designed to hold 20 passengers and there were at least 40 of us piled on board. First, I almost get killed by a crazy security guard and now I am taking my life in my own hands by riding in a bus that could break down or capsize at any moment. The stench of the bus from the diesel fumes was enough to make me almost lose it. I bit my lower lip and told myself I would get through this without getting sick.

Traffic back to the hotel was slow and terrifying. I kept looking at the photo of the Darcy's boxes I snapped with my cell phone as I was leaving. I realized at that moment that I was on the defensive and I really didn't know how to do that. I was a good kid, a good student and rose quickly to store manager at Darcy's. Then I was promoted to corporate. And even though I knew these things, I was doubting myself even with that photo in hand.

When I walked into the lobby of the hotel the front desk manager looked at me as if to see if I belonged. I literally ran to the elevator without stopping. As I entered my room, there was an envelope that had been slipped under the door. As I read the message, my heart sunk.

"Reese, this is Sandy. I'm not sure where you were today, but we toured the factory and plan to proceed with the order." Not good. "We have another day of business to conduct here and I've arranged for an airline ticket to be delivered to the hotel for you tonight. I understand it was a late night and I'm sure you'll be happy to get home. I'll speak to you when I return to Seattle." Worse.

Three flights and more than 24 hours later, I touched down in Seattle. I hardly knew what day it was, let alone the time. It was dark, cold wet and depressing. I took my bag up to the loft and went back downstairs to hide my misery in a plate of spaghetti and red sauce.

"Where have you been? You look exhausted," exclaimed Carmine. He put a glass of wine in front of me before I could get my coat off, and then took the seat next to me. "What ails you, dear Reese?"

I took two big gulps of wine. "I blew it." He stared at me for the longest time.

After what seemed like hours, he got up and went to the kitchen, returning with a bowl of my comfort food. "Eat and then tell me what that means."

I shared my trip as if it were the reading of my diary, sparing no details or thoughts. As he listened, I could see him making mental notes of things he'd say when I was finished. He never interrupted me and when I was done, he simply said, "There are a million strange things going on, but remember that knowledge is power. You have that photo. It will all be fine."

It was getting late and he'd sat with me for a long time, so I knew he had to get back to his real job. I thanked him for listening and finished the wine that he poured into my empty glass.

I went up to my loft, too tired to even unpack. I just knew I needed to crawl into bed and shake my fears. Tomorrow would be interesting.

Chapter 15

The next morning, the entire floor was eerily quiet. Sandy had obviously not returned yet and there was no sign of Christine on the floor. The rest of the team was nowhere to be found. I sat at my desk and was dreading my meeting with Sandy upon her return.

Deep in thought, I heard Jason's voice. "Reese, wake up. I know you are probably suffering from jet lag, but I want to hear all about the trip."

I told him.

"So you were kicked off the bus, as they say."

"I guess you could say that. I really don't know if that means I am about to be fired or if they really did have other things to do."

"Who knows, but I doubt that after Sandy brought you here just a few months ago that she would suddenly eliminate your position. Just do what I do and keep your head down, and focus on that which will result in the least amount of controversy." After giving me these pearls of wisdom, Jason left my desk rather abruptly, almost as if he was afraid that if he stayed around me he would catch something.

I just couldn't get that warehouse with the Darcy pallets out of my mind. I had followed the address that had been given to me by Harry so I decided I would at least check with him to see if that warehouse was legit. I verified that I still had the picture of the Darcy pallets on my phone and decided I would go straight to Harry's office.

Walking toward the staircase with my head down, totally focused on what I would say to Harry, I bumped right into Bill. "Whoa, Reese look out! You could hurt yourself on these curvy stairs." For once Bill was not racing down the hall but was actually taking the time to make sure I was okay. I was totally embarrassed. Just one more klutzy maneuver on my part.

"I am sorry. I am probably still recovering from my whirlwind trip to Vietnam."

"Oh, that's right. You went with Clark and Sandy. How was the trip? Did you find out what was causing the quality problem with the clothes?"

Great. How do I respond to this question? Tell him that I was totally incompetent and did not find my way to even see the inside of the warehouse with the rest of the team. That would probably ensure that my head would be on the chopping block even before Sandy got back.

"I guess Sandy and Clark are happy with the factory so they are giving the approval for the spring order." I tap-danced around the issue. "I got separated from them and as a result I really don't know what they saw at the factory. For some reason the address I had did not seem to be the spot that they went to. I am on my way to talk to Harry to get his insight as to why I had the wrong address."

"I hope they discovered what was causing all of the issues. We have been besieged with customer complaints regarding the Christmas merchandise and I do not want to deal with those same issues with the spring lineup. I am free at four today, so why don't you stop by my office and give me your download on the trip."

Oh great. I have just walked into another potential political mess. This did not seem to be following Jason's advice to keep my head down and stay out of controversial issues. "Okay" was all I could say.

If anything, the piles of paper in Harry's office had gotten deeper since I had last visited him. Harry looked up at me from staring at his computer screen and had a look of surprise that someone would just walk into his domain. "Reese, you startled me. I am not used to someone just walking into my office. The normal protocol is to ask for an appointment and meet in some neutral territory like a conference room."

"Sorry Harry. I was just concerned about my recent trip and I wanted to talk to you right away about it. Somehow I have not gotten into the rhythm as to how meetings are supposed to occur around here."

"That's OK. Come on in. You are lucky that with everyone seeming to be traveling this week, I have some free time right now to talk. How was your trip?"

"I have to say the trip was one word. Weird. Nothing seemed to be what I expected."

"You have to realize you were traveling to another country and my impression is that you are not a sophisticated international traveler." That confirmed my impression of Harry that he probably was the master of understatement.

"I know, but first tell me about Juan Gomez and what he gets out of doing business with us."

"Well, as I told you, Juan was a friend of Clark's. An agent is responsible for finding manufacturers to produce the goods that we order. He will get paid by us based on the size of the order and in probability he also will get paid by the company he is representing for bringing our business to them. The Christmas business was his proving ground and the real money for him will be in delivering the spring order."

"How much are we actually spending for the spring order?"

"I really should not be telling you that as it is pretty confidential information and I am not sure if you are allowed to have that level of knowledge."

"Come on, Harry. Just give me a ball park. I promise I am not going to the press to give out this number."

"Let's just say this order is in the upper eight figures. It will require Clark's signature on the purchase order to execute the size of it. We have never made this large of an order through one agent or manufacturer before. So now you see why Clark was so intent upon traveling to Vietnam to check it out."

Now I was even more nervous. "Harry, that address you gave me—was that the actual manufacturing warehouse or just a shipping and administrative center?"

"It should have been the actual manufacturing center. My research showed that this company does everything—production, shipping, and administrative functions—all in one location. Why, wasn't that the place that you all went to check out the clothes?"

"For some reason I got separated from everyone else, which was kind of my experience the entire trip. I am not really sure where they went to check out the manufacturing. However, I was not with them. I guess I will have to wait until Sandy gets back and compare notes."

"Interesting. Well keep me informed. I got the authorization from Clark to proceed with the order and I need to get this paperwork processed so that the clothes will arrive on time in the stores."

I left Harry's office more confused than ever. *What is going on?* Not just the large clothing order, but all of the dynamics I saw overseas between Sandy and Clark, and Christine and Juan. I needed to go back to my desk and think this all through so I would know how to recap the meeting with Bill in the next hour.

Chapter 16

"Come on in, Reese. Have a seat and tell me your impressions of Vietnam." Bill got up from behind his desk and sat in one of the two chairs in his office. His office was bright and cheerful with a gorgeous view of the Puget Sound from his window. Today it was actually sunny. *How can he get anything done here?* I would be spending all of my time staring out of the window and looking at the waterfront.

I sat. "Vietnam was hot, muggy and beautiful all at the same time. Have you ever been there?"

"No, most of my travels are here in the U.S. and Canada, finding the new locations for Darcy stores. When I have vacation time the last thing I want to do is to get on a plane and fly somewhere. Now Clark has traveled everywhere. I think he would love to expand our brand overseas."

"Wow that would be exciting to open stores overseas. Do you think that will happen?"

"I did not think we would ever grow to one thousand stores, so to say that we won't expand internationally would be short-sighted on my part. When Clark sets his mind on something he has a way to make it happen. So tell me about the manufacturing plant in Hoi An."

Bill had such a way to make me feel comfortable that I found myself telling him about all of my adventures. He just listened to me intently and did not interrupt. He took a few notes as I showed him the pictures of the Darcy pallets.

"Well I heard from Clark and it seems he is comfortable to go ahead with the order. I guess we will just have to wait until they return to hear what they saw in the plant itself. Meanwhile you should probably develop the training program for the proper handling of customer cash refunds. We need to make sure that the high amount of cash refunds is not a training issue."

Bill returned to his desk. He was looking at his computer screen as if to see where he was supposed to be next. Dismissed again.

"Okay Bill, will do." Somehow in spite of Bill taking the time to talk to me I felt that I had let him down by not knowing what was going on. I decided to drop this quality issue in spite of the nagging thoughts in the back of my head, follow Jason's

advice and develop the training program that Bill requested.

Chapter 17

Two mornings later, I saw that there were lights on in Sandy's office. It looks like today will be the day of reckoning between Sandy and me about whether I'll keep my job. I had not heard from her since that cryptic note I received in Hoi An. Somehow not hearing from her was worse than being chewed out by her. My imagination was working overtime as to what our first conversation was going to be like.

She saw me in the doorway. "Come in, Reese."

"Sandy, about the manufacturing visit, I went to the plant but I did not see you or the rest of the team..."

"Reese, I do not understand why you went to the manufacturing site on your own. Why weren't you in the lobby at seven o'clock and ready to make the trip with the rest of us? I know you were with Christine and Juan the night before so I assumed that you knew when we were meeting. I am really disappointed in your lack of following through with meetings and lack of professionalism that you exhibited throughout the entire trip."

I was flabbergasted at this statement. Christine had specifically told me to go on my own. I knew she resented my role but I did not think she would set me up for failure. "Sandy, I thought I was supposed to go to the manufacturing plant on my own. I had the address from Harry so I did not think there would be any problems." In my usual way, I am meticulous about these kinds of details, so this was really a head scratcher for me.

"Well, obviously you had the wrong address. We saw a facility that was already beginning the production of the spring line even though we had not given them the order yet. It seemed very new, clean, and well organized with all of the employees actively involved in the process. After seeing this I was embarrassed to talk to them about the quality issues that you said had been occurring. I believe that the high cost of returns for the Christmas items was a storewide execution issue and not a sign of quality problems."

I showed Sandy the pictures on my phone of the plant that I had visited. "Those pictures don't look like anything we saw," Sandy said. "Most likely these are recycled Darcy pallets at a secondary facility. I am through talking about this with you. Bill told me that he asked you to develop a training program for the stores on handling returns. Please finish that task. I also would like to have you help Christine and the rest of the team with their expense reports. I think that you need to focus on administrative functions for the time being while you learn how to manage yourself within this office."

I sheepishly left her office, my eyes brimming with tears. All of this seemed so unfair and I felt so helpless. I could not even think straight much less do any more work that day. I decided that I needed to get out of the office immediately before I ran into Christine and totally lost it with her.

Chapter 18

Writing the training program for accepting product returns has to be the most boring job known to mankind. I had been staring at my computer and sitting in meetings for the past week, feeling like I have made no progress at all. It could be because I feel that the stores never pay any attention to a training program that comes from the corporate office. When I called Michael to ask his advice, in case I was missing something, he couldn't understand why I was wasting my time on this project. "You know that training programs just gather dust and sit on the shelf," he said. "If you want to be helpful, fix the problem of the poorly manufactured clothes so that we will not get so many returns."

"I know Michael, but I am in a political firestorm right now. No one wants to believe that there is an overarching quality issue and everyone wants to blame training as the root cause for high returns."

"Oh, well, I am glad you are at corporate and not me."

Shortly after I hung up, I saw Juan walking down the hall towards Christine's office. Sarah had just stopped by my cubicle and saw him at the same moment that I did. "Who is that adorable guy walking into Christine's office?" she said.

I looked at her in amazement. "First of all, I have never seen you excited about a guy. And second of all, you mean you have never met him?"

"Come on, Reese, I can get just excited as the next girl when I see a guy that cute. No, I haven't met him, so who is he?"

"That's Juan Gomez, the manufacturing agent who is coordinating the spring lineup."

"Oh, I heard about him, but I was not in the office when he originally came to town. Isn't he the one that is a friend of Clark's?"

I walked up to him. "Hi, Juan, what brings you to Seattle?"

"Oh, hi, Reese. I am in the country on other business and thought I would stop by and see how everything was progressing from your end for the spring season. Obviously I didn't tell Christine I was coming and I must have missed her."

"Yes she is out of town on store tours with Sandy. Is there anything I can do to help you?"

"Well, you could go to dinner with me tonight."

Dinner with Juan. That would be perfect. Not only is he cute, but I could find out from him how the manufacturing of clothes works in Vietnam. I have to admit that the thought of how jealous Christine would be also seemed like fun. So I said yes.

"Why don't you meet me at my hotel? We could get a drink and then have dinner. I would love to catch up with you and see what has been going on since you left Hoi An. I am staying at the Four Seasons on First Avenue."

After exchanging contact info Juan left the building. Sarah had overheard our entire conversation. "I am so jealous of you," she said. "Having drinks and dinner with that hunk sounds awesome. Times like these I really miss being free even though I adore my children."

I have to admit I was excited about the possibility of being alone with Juan and experiencing the food at the Four Seasons.

I left work early to get ready for my "date." I knew I was competing with Christine, so I had to think about what to wear. As I was leaving the building, I remembered a little boutique store near my apartment. I had been in there a few times but never felt justified buying anything. Tonight however was not the night for Darcy's clothes and I needed something new.

I walked into the store and talked to Karan, the owner. "I have an important date in the next hour and nothing in my closet seems to be right. Can you help me?"

She magically found just the right dress and accessories for my dinner. I bought a royal blue shift dress with a multicolored jacket. Along with heels and the perfect silver necklace. This outfit really made me feel like I could handle anything. Except the credit card bill I now had from my purchase!

Chapter 19

When I walked into the lobby of the Four Seasons, I knew I wasn't in Minot, North Dakota anymore. To call the lobby gorgeous was a massive understatement. The artwork on the walls looked like it came right from a museum, while the marble floors reflected the beautiful light that was cast from the chandeliers. In the center of the lobby was the most outstanding floral arrangement that I had ever seen. It was on a round stone table and was at least four feet tall. It was a combination of birds of paradise, orchids and twisted branches. I wanted to take my phone out of my purse and take a picture of it but I knew that I needed to act like I was used to all of this opulence. I stared at the arrangement intently committing it to memory so that I could write home and tell my mom all about it.

As I was taking in my surroundings, I heard my name called out. I looked up and there was Juan looking as beautiful as ever. "It is so good to see you. That dress is stunning," he said. "Thank you so much for taking time out of your schedule to have dinner with me. I so hate to eat alone when I am traveling. Come with me and let's be seated." Juan gently put his hand across the small of my back and guided me to the dining room.

If I thought the lobby of the hotel was glamorous, the dining room was equally beautiful. It was surrounded by glass with the view of the Puget Sound. The maître 'de sat us right by the window, just in time for a spectacular sunset. I was really spellbound by all of the beauty and being with this amazing man. I needed to get my wits together so that I could find out what I wanted to know about the manufacturing process.

"Tell me what have you been up to since you came back from Viet Nam," Juan said. "I was sorry that you did not join us for the tour of the manufacturing facility. Christine told me that you were feeling the effects of our toasts of rice wine from the night before. I am so sorry. I should have warned you that rice wine has a way of sneaking up on you."

I couldn't believe she had said this to him—especially since it was not true. But I knew that if I was too indignant, it would only ruin my chance to find out more information.

"Somehow our communication was mixed up," I said. "I am sorry I did not go with the rest of the team and obviously I went to the wrong location when I tried to go to the plant on my own."

"Hoi An can be a very confusing place to find your way around in. Now tell me what are you working on?"

I proceeded to tell him about my dealings with the training program. I tried not to show how bored I was with the project, but I am sure he could tell I was less than enthused. The conversation then moved onto our respective families and his background growing up in California. His mother was from Mexico and met his father when he was in the military.

"How did you get to know Clark?" I said.

"He and I went to school together. I was on a basketball scholarship and Clark was one of our biggest fans. He knew how much I needed to keep my grades up to stay in school and keep my scholarship so he would help me study for exams. Clark always has had a love for basketball. "

"When I was traveling with him once I watched him watch two games at the same time. I don't think I have ever seen anyone do that before," Juan continued.

"Yes; I think basketball is a great stress reliever for him. Enough about Clark, let's order dinner."

The evening proceeded with Juan was amazing company. There wasn't a topic that he was not able to talk about. But as the evening came to an end, he totally took me off guard with his next statement.

"I have really enjoyed being with you tonight," he said, "and I would love to continue our conversation in my room. Now before you think that it is not appropriate let me tell you that I am in a suite of rooms and I really want to show you the view."

I wasn't born yesterday and I knew what he was really saying, but the truth is, I wanted to have the evening go on and so I probably did the most inappropriate thing ever. I said yes.

Juan's suite of rooms was on the twenty-fifth floor of the hotel. The beauty that I had been exposed to so far continued in his suite. Once again, it took advantage of the views of the city with floor-to-ceiling windows. The floor was a plush white carpet and the living area had a beautiful mahogany desk with a sofa and chairs strategically placed to look out on the Sound.

"Excuse me, Reese, I am going to my room for a moment. Please make yourself at home in my humble abode." With that Juan walked through the door to the adjoining bedroom.

I knew I had to capture this room with pictures and I wanted to take them quickly before he returned and caught me acting like a country girl who is just visiting the city. I began snapping shots as fast as possible with my phone. I noticed that there was a pile of papers on the desk so I thought I would capture this also to show that he really did work in this suite of rooms and not just play Casanova.

I had just put my phone back in my purse when Juan walked back into the main suite. He walked over to the minibar and opened the small refrigerator removing a bottle of champagne. "I think we need to toast our newfound friendship," he said. He smoothly opened the bottle as if he had been doing this his entire life. We sat on the couch, sipping the most beautiful champagne while admiring the clear night sky. I was in heaven. The next thing I knew he put his glass down and reached over and kissed me.

I don't know if it was his smoothness, the effects of the champagne, or just the ambience of the moment but that kiss was the most sensual kiss I had experienced in ages. All thoughts about talking about work completely left my addled brain. Juan leaned back. "I have wanted to do that all night. I hope you are not offended."

Offended! I was in heaven and wanted him to continue.

I had just turned to him to continue this ecstasy when a shrieking alarm pierced the sound barrier of the room, followed by the blare of a loudspeaker.

"*This is a fire alarm. Please leave your rooms immediately and gather outside the building. We repeat, this is a fire alarm.*" Juan and I looked at each other and burst out laughing. Of all times for a fire alarm to go off. It was almost as if someone was watching over me and knew that they needed to interrupt my evening right then. We knew that as much as we wanted to ignore the warning, we couldn't, so we gathered up our things and headed for the door. I noticed that Juan was careful to collect the papers on his desk and put them in his briefcase.

After walking down twenty-five flights of stairs, we gathered outside with the other guests as firefighters entered the hotel. Juan and I stood under a nearby canopy of an adjacent building and watched the commotion.

"This was not how I wanted our evening to end," Juan said. I nodded, but some part of me knew that the alarm probably saved me from doing something stupid. "We need to get together again. Perhaps in Viet Nam?"

"I don't think that I will be back in Viet Nam in the near future," I said.

"Just leave that to me. If you would like to come back to see me, I can make sure that it happens." He seemed awfully confident about a return trip and I wasn't sure why; but there was something in the way he looked at me that made me feel full of anticipation.

"Of course I would love to come back and see you, but don't underestimate how upset Sandy was with me after the last trip."

"Let's not ruin the night with talking about that right now," Juan said. "I am going to find you a taxi so that you can return home, and I will see you in Hoi An in the near future. Trust me on that."

Right at that moment a cab came down the street and Juan let out a piercing whistle to get its attention. "I didn't tell you that I had worked as a bellboy in my early years. Hailing a cab effectively was a job requirement," he said with a smile. He opened the door for me and as I got in the cab, he leaned in and gave me a chaste kiss goodnight. "See you in Viet Nam," he said as he closed the door. How he was going to pull that off was beyond me but I decided to sit back and enjoy the ride.

Chapter 20

It had only been a few weeks since I'd been to yoga, but it felt more like months. I had no idea if I could even balance anymore—good thing I can always stay in child's pose if not. I also wasn't sure I wanted to run into Dan. Our great afternoon in Seattle was so long ago that it's almost been forgotten, and he never followed up. But that's not why I need to go to yoga. I made a promise to myself that I'd go regularly and I have to make good on that promise.

I arrived at the studio just in time to grab the last spot, way in the back of the crowded room. Sitting, eyes closed, I made a valiant attempt to decompress and regulate my breathing before the instructor asked us to stand. The next thing I heard was Dan's voice, up front—he was teaching the class tonight. My overwhelming urge to flee was quickly quashed when Dan, during his welcoming remarks, said, "And it's nice to have Reese back with us again."

I gave a brief smile but I didn't make eye contact with him, or anyone. Mostly, I just started straight ahead, hoping and praying that he wouldn't make me feel like more of a spectacle than I already did. He seemed to pick up on that from me, because other than a few corrections during class, he said nothing more until I was in the studio lobby, grabbing an updated schedule.

"Well, hello, stranger. Have you been avoiding me, yoga, or both?"

Neither. I was off in Vietnam where I managed to screw up royally and then I was at the Four Seasons being kissed by a business colleague. But I simply smiled and said, "Nice to see you, too." I felt sarcasm as I said those words, but Dan didn't seem to take it that way.

"Well, I'm glad you're back. Do you have time for a bowl of Pho?"

I was tired and really wanted to sit on my couch with a glass of wine. And I wasn't in the mood to talk about work. "It sounds yummy but I'm exhausted from work. Perhaps another time?"

"Sounds fair. Name the when and I'll pick the place."

My mind on Juan, I wasn't sure if I wanted to see him again, but in the moment I blurted out, "Friday?" While that sounded desperate when it came out of my mouth, my brain was actually working overtime. It was Wednesday—I figured he'd already have plans and then I could avoid it for a while. I had plans with Jack and Carey on Saturday, so that would buy me some time.

"Perfect. Let's meet at seven at Carmine's for a glass of wine. I like their food but there is this cute little place in Pioneer Square that I've wanted to try. A friend of a friend is the hostess, so I'll get us a reservation. It's casual. See you then."

As he did so well, Dan smiled and turned to walk out of the studio. I sort of stood there wondering why my compulsion to say "yes" was so strong these days. All of this was testing my sense of comfort.

Chapter 21

I arrived about ten minutes early, hoping to catch Carmine and clue him into my evening. I figured otherwise he would give Dan the third degree and embarrass me. The bar was quieter than usual for a Friday night, but the rain was coming down in sheets and likely keeping tourists in their downtown hotels rather than venturing out. Of course, as I thought about guests in their hotels, I couldn't help but remember being in Juan's hotel room … sigh. I needed to get him out of my mind, at least for tonight.

I found two seats, put my coat on the empty one and plopped onto the bar stool. Carmine caught me out of the corner of my eye, walked out from behind the counter and gave me a big hug.

"You look great, Reese—a little tired, perhaps—but I see a gleam in your eyes." I was just about to give him the 411 on Dan when Dan arrived. I could see instantly that Carmine thought Dan was responsible for the gleam, which was the last thing I wanted. Not only would Dan get endless questions, I was going to be put on the spot with Carmine's silliness. Great.

Dan came over and said hello to me. But before he could even sit on the bar stool, Carmine extended his hand. "Welcome to Carmine's. Any friend of Reese's is a friend of mine—she is like family to me!"

I sat there with a smirk. Family? That was pretty cool. Dan handled it well. "Nice to meet you," he said, then turned to me. "You look great. It's nice to see you tonight."

The skeptical side of me thought he was doing this for Carmine's benefit, but Dan has been pretty easygoing and free with the compliments. I decided to take it at face value. "It's nice to see you, too."

I don't remember ordering but two glasses of red wine appeared in front of us. Dan graciously thanked Carmine and raised a glass to toast to "new friendships." I took a rather large sip of wine and because I had not bothered to eat lunch, it went right to my head. This was a good thing. I was finally able to relax a little. Dan shared what he'd been up to since the last time we'd gone out. His work and family are interesting, and he was easy to converse with.

After about forty-five minutes, he told me it was time to go to dinner and we both stood. Carmine came racing over to say the wine was on the house—no arguing—but Dan did leave him a nice tip anyway. Dan helped me into my coat, and off we went.

Pioneer Square was the center of Seattle at one time, but somehow earned a bad reputation for too many bars, unsavory transients and dying businesses. So many of the buildings have unique architecture both inside and out. Many of them have become dilapidated over the years, but one by one, they have been reopening as cocktail bars, restaurants and local-merchant shops.

The restaurant was the corner of King and Occidental. Occidental on this block does not allow cars, giving it much more of a plaza than street feel. The building was small, but it had the most amazing sculptured ceiling, as well as beautiful fixtures and a warm feel. We were a few minutes early for our reservation and walked over to the standing bar to wait.

The kitchen was open and made for great theater. Dan and I had a great time watching the chefs prepare dishes. Of course I wanted everything I saw coming out of the kitchen, and we had a good laugh wondering how much we could actually eat.

He was asking me about work when the hostess came to seat us.

The table was perfect, with views of the kitchen and bar that we were both able to enjoy. As starving as we were, we decided to share a few small plates and split one entrée. Fortunately, our tastes in food were similar –We split charred octopus with white beans and roasted red peppers, tuna ceviche with a wasabi avocado "frosting" and a frisee salad with lardons and poached egg for starters, followed by chicken with shishito peppers and a house aioli. We drank a glass of Syrah while we ate and the conversation seemed to easily flow. Dan had a way of making me feel comfortable without being patronizing.

I told him all about my trip to Vietnam, including the debacle about visiting the factory, and he listened intently. I left nothing out when I told him about the armed guard and I think he was scared for me. He asked lots of questions about Vietnam as if he was trying to paint a mental picture of the country. He was fascinated by the cultural nuances I described, and wanted to know all about the food, too.

The conversation turned to him and how his work was going. I realized that he didn't often talk about it and I asked why. He was funny and simply said, "Remember, I told you that it's just work. I love what I do but when I leave it, it's off my mind. I don't ever want to confuse work with the rest of my life."

That struck an immediate chord in me, and my mind drifted off to Juan. As the server cleared our plates, Dan pulled me out of my trance by asking if I wanted dessert.

"You seem miles away all of a sudden, as if you were reminiscing about Vietnam," he said.

He was right. "It was an amazing trip, I met some wonderful people but it was also weird." I stopped there but Dan pushed me to explain.

"What's troubling you about the trip?"

As we shared this amazing walnut tart for dessert, I explained briefly that my co-workers seemed to mix business with their personal lives more than I thought. "I am not suspicious by nature but they seem to act like better friends than colleagues at times. The local agent and my colleague and sometimes nemesis seem close, but I think she's more interested in him than he is in her."

"It sounds a little mysterious to me, Reese. And also a little nefarious. If I understand it right, this agent is making a large fee from this business deal. His incentive to wine and dine is pretty clear, and it sounds like he'd do whatever he had to in order to secure the business."

Now I was annoyed. He was clearly criticizing Juan and insinuating that Juan's feelings weren't real. I was confused as to why I was mad—after all, I didn't want Juan to have real feelings for Christine. But I realized that I was taking it personally. I don't know what would have happened if the fire alarm hadn't gone off, but why else would Juan want me back in Vietnam? He had the business and received his fee, so he didn't need me at all. I just knew he was being genuine.

"Well, I don't know to be honest," I said after gathering my thoughts. "He seemed like a smart and savvy businessman, and he's friends with our CEO. I just don't think he'd do anything to jeopardize that relationship and risk future business."

"You may be right. You said everyone was having after-dinner drinks and maybe things aren't as they seemed. Are you upset by this conversation? I don't want to ruin a perfectly nice evening."

Dan had this way of calming me down and putting the focus back on to the good things without ignoring what I say. In that moment, he brought me back from drifting into thoughts of Juan.

We had a nightcap—decaf for me, espresso for Dan. Dan turned the conversation away from work and asked me how much time I'd spent on any of the islands in Puget Sound, particularly Bainbridge Island. I had not.

"I'd like to spend a day with you there sometime," Dan said. "It's got a few wineries, cute restaurants and the views are amazing. It's a ferry ride away and worth the trip, especially on a nice day."

"You know, I'd like that. But how do you ever plan for weather in Seattle?"

He chuckled, knowing that one of the great things about Seattle is that it will sometimes rain while the sun is out. "Well, hopefully we'll get lucky."

I offered to split the check and after some negotiation, he allowed me to leave the tip. I still wasn't sure what "this" was, but I know I didn't want him to always feel obligated to pay. Funny, I didn't feel that way at all about Juan.

He walked me back to my loft. The rain had stopped and the smell of marine air was intoxicating. Maybe that's why as I got out my key and said turned to thank him, he moved as if to kiss me. I was a little stunned and taken aback, and knew it was because I had just kissed Juan days ago.

Dan looked confused and then instantly embarrassed, immediately apologizing.

"You just startled me, that's all." The truth was, I really wanted it to be Juan. Now I was embarrassed. An uncomfortable few seconds that felt like hours passed. I felt sheepish and weird, so I hugged him. "I look forward to going to Bainbridge."

"Me, too." We exchanged numbers. I thanked him again, squeezed his hand and went upstairs.

I was completely confused as I sat on my couch. This guy was nice, respectful, funny, and smart, and lives in Seattle. He's not connected to work and we seem to have a great time. But isn't something starting with Juan? He's so different and I know he has feelings for me. And he's not slimy at all—that was just Dan being jealous. Yet he's literally miles away, and older and more experienced than I am.

Good thing I'm seeing Jack and Carey tomorrow night. They'll help me figure it out.

Chapter 22

I slept in, did laundry and was feeling sort of lazy, even though I was really looking forward to seeing my friends and getting some sort of relief from my state of confusion. I dated a bit in college but was too focused on my grades and making money at Darcy's, so I'm not well versed in this at all. That said, I knew what it was like to feel that pitter-patter of excitement, and now it had happened with two different men in the past few months. Weird.

It was good to be at Jack and Carey's. Jack is an amazing cook and I'd cancel plans to eat anything he made. I hadn't had Mexican in forever and all of a sudden, I was starving. "I'd love to, Jack; what can I do to help?"

"You know, this is therapy for me. It's been incredibly political at work, but we finally will get the West Seattle project done. It's been a great lesson in balancing professional ethics with business savvy, and I am really pleased I was able to navigate through. Once I reminded myself that it was about the school and the kids, and not about me personally, I was fine. Great life lesson."

I so appreciated how Jack could distill issues down to simple ideas that were really smart. I'm not sure how he is in matters of the heart, but he's great at business perspective.

Jack went back to chopping and stirring, and I settled on the couch with the Times front page. It was rare that I sat and read a real newspaper. I thought I should try to do this more often, but I knew I was kidding myself. I never sat that long.

Just as I was in the middle of reaching about the waterfront tunnel woes, Carey came bounding through the door with a can of chipotles and a twelve pack of Modelo Negro. I'm so glad I can walk home from there.

Carey, who had finally been hired by the Seattle Police Department, was excited to share her police academy stories with me. "I'm exhausted from all the boot-camp activities and I'm literally starving all the time," she said, "but I'm having fun and the classroom work is really interesting. It's funny, I am really intrigued by the criminal work and am seriously considering the detective track as my emphasis."

I was expecting Jack to say something about that, but silence hung in the air.

"I know it's scary, but Ann Rule has always been somewhat of a folk hero to me, and she did know Ted Bundy. That's just cool."

"You've got moxie, Carey. I am not sure I'd be up to that challenge."

"As if you don't have it in a similar but different way in the corporate world. I listen to Jack talk about work and I don't think I could ever be savvy enough to put up with all the politics. On the street, it is survival – and I know I have that instinct."

As the sauce simmered, Jack opened three beers and sat with us. "So Reese, what's new?"

It wasn't like Jack to be that direct with me because Carey typically beat him to the punch. While I thought it was odd, I was glad he opened up the subject. I proceeded to tell them all about my trip to Vietnam, being extra sure to not miss one single detail. There were lots of questions, especially about my trip to the factory. Carey was going to make a great detective!

At some point, the sun went down. Jack assembled the enchiladas and came back with the second round of beers. He was smart enough to bring some chips and salsa, too. "So do you think that there is anything going on between Sandy and Clark, or Christine and Juan?" he asked. "It just seems like there were some unspoken things that happened."

"I don't know about Clark and Sandy, but there is absolutely nothing going on between Juan and Christine," I said defiantly.

"Whoa, I didn't mean to offend you. I just asked a simple question."

At that point, I decided to share the story of my date with Juan.

"Sadly, he sent me home in a cab," I finished "but has assured me he will bring me back to Vietnam to see him."

Dead silence. Carey and Jack stared at one another, each waiting for the other to say something. As I was about to break the ice, Carey turned toward me.

"Seriously, Reese. You don't know this man at all, he is heavily involved with your company and your team, and you go to his hotel room? What were you thinking?"

"Why do you think you can trust this man? It's like playing with fire," Jack added. "And what about your date with yoga guy last night?"

I wasn't sure what surprised me more—their misplaced disdain for Juan or the fact that they knew I'd been out with Dan. I knew they were being protective of me, but I was still caught off guard and pretty uncomfortable.

"My date?"

"You're not the only one who eats at Carmine's. We went there for a late dinner and he told us all about chatting with you and Dan before you ran off somewhere else for dinner."

"Dan is a nice guy, but I think just a friend. He's still in law school and has a very busy life. And Juan gives me butterflies—is that so bad?"

"It's not about bad. The operative word is 'smart'." When you first told us about Dan, you seemed excited and you've had two really great dates with him. He's not entangled in your work and seems like an honest, nice guy. That is what I mean by smart."

I could see I was fighting a losing battle. "I know it sounds rather spontaneous and not like me, but I can't help how I feel. And I probably won't get to go back to Vietnam since I'm low person on the totem pole now, so it's not worth discussing. Thanks for listening."

"He sounds slimy to me, Reese, and men don't usually call other men slimy."

"Okay, you two," Carey cut in. "The table is set and the enchiladas have settled. Let's eat and talk about something else."

With that, we ate and finished the rest of the twelve pack. As we ate, we chatted about Carmine, a movie they had seen recently, and what they were thinking about in terms of a trip during Carey's academy break.

"Thanks for an amazing dinner as always, Jack; it was great to just hang out and talk. Next time, I'm cooking."

As Jack helped me with my coat, he simply said, "I look forward to it. Walk home safely and be smart."

I understood his message, even though I wasn't happy that he had the last word.

Chapter 23

At my desk at work on Monday I could not get Jack's words out about Juan of my head. Part of me was frustrated at Carey and Jack for being so judgmental about Juan without even meeting him, while the other part had to admit they had some good points.

As I was staring at my computer trying to finish up that stupid training package, I received a message from Sandy—she wanted to meet with me at ten o'clock. What could this be about? She had been so silent and reserved around me ever since our trip that I thought she did not know that I existed any more.

I gathered up my notebook and trudged off to Sandy's office. This would probably be another "make work" project. I was looking at my feet and almost ran into Christine as she was departing the office. "Sorry," I said and Christine just gave me a glare and walked back off toward her office. *Wow, what was that all about?*

"Come in Reese. Have a seat." Sandy was exceedingly friendly and courteous. "How has the training program been progressing?"

"I am almost finished with it. We are scheduled to test the flow next week."

"Good. I think you should turn this over to Sarah. I have something else I need you to focus on."

I wanted to jump up and give anyone around me a high-five. But I am trying to show more maturity so I just looked up from my notebook. "Okay, but can I ask why?"

"Juan reached out to Clark and requested assistance from us to set up the administrative details for the shipment of the product for the spring line. Since we have never purchased such a large order from one supplier, he wants to make sure that all the details for the initial shipment are taken care of. "

"I will be happy to help but I am curious why you are talking to me rather than to Christine about this."

"I would have reached out to Christine, but Juan seems to have the idea that you are more qualified to help him on this project. He told Clark that Christine was better suited for developing the next line of fashion while he thought you would be more detail oriented to set up these administrative details. It seemed strange to me that he would be that familiar with your skill set. Did you have any contact with him since our past trip?"

"Just briefly last week when you and Christine were on store tours. He was in the office looking for the two of you and since you were not here, we met for dinner. He wanted to know why I had not met you all for the tour of the manufacturing plant in Hoi An."

"Oh, that explains why he mentioned you to Clark."

"What do you need me to do?"

"You will need to go back to Vietnam and help him arrange for the shipping procedure back to the states in time for the spring launch. I want to avoid having to ship this much product by air in order to avoid a cost overrun. I suggest that you reach out to Juan and set up your travel schedule accordingly. See if you can't act more professionally on this trip and not miss scheduled meetings."

Ouch, that barb hurt! "I won't let you down. Thanks, Sandy, for giving me this chance."

"You should thank Juan and Clark. I am still skeptical that you have the maturity to pull this off. Needless to say, this assignment will be very important for you in terms of your career at Darcy's."

With those less-than-inspiring words, I exited her office.

As I walked to back to my cube, I heard Christine call my name from her office. "Reese, can you come in here please?" I walked to her office and she looked at me with a sweet smile on her face. I knew something must be up, since she had totally ignored me since we returned from Vietnam.

"I talked to Juan and he told me that he had requested that you come over to Vietnam to set up the shipping instructions for the spring line. I am so glad he asked for you, since that task is so tedious and boring."

"I really don't understand why I need to go back to Hoi An to set up this process."

"I think it is just to make Clark comfortable that someone from Darcy's will actually be in country to set up the details rather than relying entirely on third parties. I just wanted you to know that if you need anything, just give me a call."

After she had previously misled everyone about why I had not made the initial manufacturing visit, Christine would be the last person I would call if I needed anything. "Sure, will do," I replied, trying to sound as gracious as possible.

One thing about working in the corporate office if you are doing something at the request of top management, it is amazing how fast the bureaucracy disappears. I had my travel arrangements for a return trip to Vietnam set up and confirmed by the end of the day.

Chapter 24

The airport in Da Nang was as hot and humid as the first time I was here. Juan was waiting for me at baggage claim. He was as amazing looking as ever. Somehow the heat does not seem to bother him. I, on the other hand, feel like I am going to wilt away.

He grabbed my arm and began to pull me through the throngs in the airport lobby. "What's the rush?" I said. "You are pulling my arm off!"

"I'm sorry, I just wanted to get out of here and back to the hotel."

"Relax, Juan. I am here just like you planned, so let's not get carried away." I had promised myself to slow things down and not do something I would later regret.

"I just found out I need to go to China tomorrow and that is the reason for the rush. I need to get you settled and up to speed on what needs to be done before I leave town."

I really felt foolish. I thought he was trying to continue where we left off in his hotel room. I needed to get my head out of the clouds and focus on the business at hand, rather than letting my imagination go overboard.

"What's going on in China?"

"Christine has found another potential manufacturer for the additional lines of clothes for Darcy's. As your agent, it's my responsibility to meet with them and check them out. The car and driver are over here."

Juan helped me navigate across the road and past the crazy drivers that were whizzing through the airport.

As we settled into the back seat of the Mercedes, I turned to Juan. "So why do you have to go to China now? I thought you were adamant that I needed to be here right away and now you are leaving."

"Sorry, but you being here allows me to leave. This way I know that you will be following up on the logistics of the distribution back to the States and I can work with Christine to ensure future orders for the company."

I looked out of the window and the passing rice paddies and thought that this really did not make sense. But I decided to just go with it.

Next thing I knew we were back in the same boutique hotel we had stayed in just a short while ago. "Miss Turnbull, it is nice to have you back with us. We have booked you into the same room you were in the last time. Please let us know if you need anything else." One thing is for sure – the service at the hotels in this country is over the top. I could definitely get used to this style of travel.

I left Juan in the lobby and arranged to meet him later for dinner so I could find out what it was that he needed me to do while I was back in Vietnam.

After a much needed shower, I came back down stairs to the infamous bar where I had drank rice wine with Christine and Juan, Juan was seated at a table—this time with a small Vietnamese woman. He waved me over. "Reese I want you to meet An Hoang." She was petite—actually shorter than me— and had coal black hair and dark brown eyes.

"Reese it is nice to meet you," she said. Juan has told me some lovely things about you." Somehow I don't think he has told her everything about me!

"An will be your assistant while you are here," Juan said. "I don't want you to have to go to the plant, so An and her brother Vinh will be at your beckon call for anything you may need. This way I know that you are being taken care of while I am in China for the next few days."

"Reese, I think we can work out of the hotel," An said. "There is a good internet connection here and I can handle any communication you may need with the plant. Not everyone at the plant is fluent in English, so we thought it would be easier if you had me to be your translator and expeditor."

I nodded. "Sounds like you two have thought of everything. I assume that Vinh was the driver that brought Juan and me to the hotel this afternoon."

"Yes, Vinh is my driver whenever I am in Hoi An." Juan responded. "I did not want you to get lost this time, so I thought that I needed to ensure that you had the necessary support."

I was relieved. "Thanks for the assistance."

"It is my pleasure. After all, it is important to me also that everything proceed with this order without any problems. Now let's order dinner."

Chapter 25

The one thing about traveling overseas that I have not grown used to is being wide awake at two in the morning. Back in the States when I wake up at this time, I usually can roll over and go right back to sleep; but here I wake up totally refreshed as if I had just finished a power nap. I decided to take advantage of my clear thinking.

I was still bothered by what I had seen at the building during my last visit. I also felt like I needed to see the manufacturing plant so that I could vouch for its quality to the store managers I had spoken with throughout my holiday phone-call project. Truth be known, I needed to make sure that I was not going crazy. The challenge would be to accomplish these tasks while Juan was away since he seems pretty adamant about me not visiting the plant. I wrote all of these ideas on a "to do" list.

I met An in the lobby of the hotel at nine a.m. "I have arranged for us to work in a conference room in this hotel," she informed me as I stepped out of the elevator. She obviously is efficient and disinclined to waste any time on idle chitchat.

"That's great," I replied as she led me to a room that looked like a prison cell.

"I felt this room would prevent us from having any distractions". An is obviously the master of understatement.

"Of course," I said." Just let me hook up my lap top and we can get started."

After working nonstop for over an hour to ensure that our spreadsheets were up to date, I looked at An. "I have to take a break."

"I am sorry," An said. "I should have anticipated that for you. I am sure you are still dealing with jet lag and this must seem tedious to you. ."

"Well it does and sitting in this room without any view is pretty claustrophobic."
"I understand. I am used to this type of environment and I forget that in the States you have larger spaces with windows."
"Well not everywhere but I guess we do get used to having more space."

"Why don't we take a break and go out of the building for lunch? That way I can show you more of Hoi An and you can have our fantastic food. My mother owns a nearby restaurant and I know she would be honored to serve you lunch."

"That would be great," I said. "I will focus on finishing up these spreadsheets so that we can enjoy the break."

Two hours later we were back in the Mercedes being chauffeured to An and Vinh's mother's restaurant. The location was hidden in the woods next to the river. An must have sensed my surprise at the location. "Hoi An is really a small town. It is totally dependent upon tourist traffic. All of the locals know about my mother's restaurant and they take their 'honored' guests here for either lunch or dinner. Being hidden away allows the tourists to feel that they are at a special location."

Inside, An's mother had already set a table for three. "If you don't mind we would like to order for you."

I nodded. That was the last decision I needed to make.

What followed was wonderful. It started with spring rolls, such a delicacy, the likes of which I had never tasted in the States. They were followed by a beautiful mango salad. The mango was as fresh as it had just been taken off the tree. We then had fried rice and the main entrée, grilled lemongrass chicken. I made a mental note to myself to remember every detail so that I could tell Carmine all about this "light" lunch when I returned home.

Throughout the entire lunch, I noticed An's mother going up to each of the tables and checking to make sure everything was to her customer's satisfaction. There must have been 50 people being serviced at the same time, but I did not see any one getting less than perfect service.

After lunch, An and Vinh suggested that we have coffee so that we could wait and meet their mother. The last thing I wanted to do was go back to that claustrophobic meeting room, so I readily agreed. "How did the two of you learn such excellent English?"

"We grew up speaking both English and Vietnamese," An said. "During the American war, our parents spent a lot of time with the American soldiers. Hoi An was a demilitarized zone so it was the R&R spot for the soldiers. Most of the fighting took place in the jungles in central Vietnam, while Da Nang was the home of the hospital for the American soldiers. Hoi An was the play spot. It was during this time that my parents opened up their restaurant."

It always seems strange to me to hear the Vietnam War being called the American War, but it makes sense once you are here. "Does your father still work in the restaurant?"

"He passed away last year. That is why Vinh and I are back in Hoi An. We both decided to return to help Mother with both the adjustment of living without our father and to manage the restaurant."

"I am sorry. I am sure that she is happy that you both are back, but from where are you back?"

"We were both attending university in the States. At some point we will go back; but for now it is important for us to help our family," Vinh responded.

At that moment their mother came to join us at our table. She was a small woman with a beautiful smile. Her hair was still coal black even though she had to be in her late sixties or early seventies. "Welcome to my restaurant. I hope you enjoyed your meal."

"The lunch was fantastic. I don't think I have ever had spring rolls so freshly made."

"I am so happy that you enjoyed it." She then sat down at our table while Vinh got up and served her a coffee. "My son and daughter do such a good job taking care of me. Now tell me what brings you to Hoi An."

"Mother I already told you that Reese is here to work with Juan to set up the distribution of the clothes that are being made at the new plant for the stores in the States."

"Oh yes," she said. "It is good to see that plant being productive again."

"What do you mean? I thought that plant had been in business for a long time." Hearing that the plant was just recently being productive made me wonder what she was talking about.

"The plant came under new management at the end of last year. I think a Chinese company bought it. Before that it was a low-production facility. Most of the employees are not from this area."

I made a decision. "Vinh and An, I know that Juan did not want us to visit the plant because he thought we had so much to do. But since we made such good progress this morning setting up the spreadsheets, could we drive by the plant this afternoon? The rest of the team visited the plant on their previous visit but I did not have a chance to see it." Their mother's words regarding the Chinese ownership and the fact that the employees were not local made me very curious to visit the plant location.

"I don't see any problem with driving by the facility," Vinh said. "I know some short cuts so we can make excellent time and still get you back to finish your distribution plans."

"Oh, thanks, Vinh. An, I will not tell Juan about this side trip so you do not have to worry about him finding out."

"All of you need to be careful around that plant. I hear they are not very welcoming to "tourists" looking at their facility." Their mother seemed to be very concerned about us spending any time near the plant. I needed to figure out how to get her to share what she knew about the plant. Just when I was going to ask the question An asked it for me. We definitely thought the same way.

"Mother how do you know this?" asked An.

"I really should not be telling you this but my close friend used to work at the plant under the old ownership. When the Chinese came in she was let go and she told me about the changes that were taking place."

"Do you think we could meet with her?" I asked.

"Why don't you visit the plant and if you still feel like you want to meet with her I will make a call. An you remember Cam Le – she was my old friend from school. You would have to go with your friend to meet with Cam and perhaps she will tell you what she knows."

With that said, we excused ourselves and headed for the car. I definitely thought that everything we had learned seemed very strange compared to what the team saw when they were here the first time. I was very anxious to see this facility.

The next thing I knew we were driving up to the same facility that I had seen on my own several weeks ago. "This can't be right. Everyone told me this address was just an administrative building and shipping location."

"No; this is the only location for the plant. That building you see behind the warehouse is the dorm where the employees live when they are not working." Vinh seemed to be very positive about his facts.

"But the team went to another location to see how the plant worked and they did not mention anything about dorms that housed employees."

"It is very common for manufacturers to set up a demonstration station to show prospective customers what they can produce. In this way they are not upsetting the normal orders that need to be delivered, but can tailor make the demo site to all of the needs of the customer." An seemed to be very confident about this practice.

"You mean they do this and do not tell anyone that it is a demo site?" I was incredulous about this deception.

"Well they should tell the customer that it is a demo site but since I was not there I cannot tell you what was said," replied An, diplomatically.

"I really need to get into that warehouse. Especially since the team has not seen these facilities."

"As you can see by the fence around the grounds, you would have a difficult time getting in without an appointment. When you were here the first time how did you get on the grounds?"

"I entered from the back of the building. At the time all I saw were pallets with the Darcy address on them. A big guard came up to me carrying a gun. He scared me off and I literally ran back to the main road."

"You are lucky that is all that happened. They are very protective of their privacy and he could have had you taken to the authorities."

"Everyone must have been at the demo site so that is why you were not stopped by a guard. As you can see that is not the case now."

As he said this, a guard approached our car. "This is private property and you need to move on." He was very fierce and had the look of someone we did not want to mess with.

I took his picture and pictures of the buildings with my phone. At the time I was taking pictures of the dorm, I captured some young plant workers heading back to their rooms. Oh no; all of this deception and potential violations of labor laws. Just what I needed to discover.

"After seeing all of this I really need to meet with your mother's friend."

"I totally understand. I will do my best to convince her to talk to you. After we get back to the hotel I will call her and see if I can get something set up."

I think that An was as surprised as I was as to what was going on. At least I have an accomplice to help me uncover this mystery.

Chapter 26

After much persuading from An, An's mother made arrangements for us to meet her friend Cam Le that evening. An and I went without Vinh, as he had other chauffeuring business he needed to take care of.

We met Cam Le at a nearby coffee shop. It seems local coffee cafes are universal around the world. We walked into the small building and saw an older heavy set woman sitting by herself at a table in the café. "Cam," An called out.

Cam looked up from her phone and a large smile crossed her face. "An, it is so good to see you. I have not seen you since your father's funeral. It appears that you and your brother being back home is just what your mother needed to get through this time."

"I know and we are happy to be here with her. How is your family?" asked An as we approached the table and pulled chairs up to join Cam Le.

"Everyone is fine. It was difficult when I lost my job at the manufacturing plant but I have found an excellent position at a local tailoring shop making suits for the tourists. It is very enjoyable as no two orders are ever alike."

"That's right this area is famous for the custom suits that can be made in a very short period of time." I said.

"Yes that helps with the attraction from the tourists especially the visitors from Australia."

"I have seen some of the suits that you have made and I am amazed that you can produce such quality in a short period of time."

"You will have to have a suit made for yourself while you are here. But An, your mother said Reese wanted to know about the manufacturing plant that I originally worked at."

"Yes. I am here from Darcy's, a clothing retailer that is based in Seattle. We have just completed an order for spring clothes from this company." I felt rather than An, I should answer this question.

As I was saying this, Cam Le looked very uncomfortable. "I had no idea that you were doing business with this company. If I had known I probably would not have agreed to talk to you. I would not want this company to know that I had shared any information with you."

"Cam, you can trust Reese. We just need to know what is going on because it does not seem that all of the facts about this operation have been shared with Darcy's." An was using her most persuasive voice to keep Cam talking to us and not leaving the café.

"Yes, Cam; I will not share your information or name with anyone."

"I am only doing this out of respect for your parents, An. I do not think that you should be involved with this company, but if you do not know the facts I guess I cannot blame you for working with them."

"Thank you Cam. So what is going on?"

"Well as you know, the Chinese have been making investments in Vietnam. In most cases they are happy to have the investment to be merely an infusion of capital; however in this case, they have not only bought out the plant, they have brought in their own employees to operate the plant. It appears that the cost of operating plants in China has escalated so they are looking for more cost effective locations in which to operate."

"You mean the employees of the plant live on site and may not be from Vietnam?" An seemed to be totally amazed about this information.

"I really don't know where they are from but yes, they do live on site and they are definitely not from this area. One of the reasons that they let all of us go when they took over is that they wanted total control of the employees at the plant."

"By total control do you mean that they may be violating some of the labor laws?" I asked hoping for a negative response.

"Since I am not there I can't tell you that for certain, however; from what I have heard from companies that are providing services to the plant, that is what is going on. In addition, they have not upgraded any of the equipment since they took over so I know that the quality of the clothes is probably not at American standards."

As Cam continued to tell us one horror story after another, all I could think of was "how was I going to prevent

Darcy's from being involved in a gigantic disaster with the

spring shipment."

Chapter 27

Back in my room, I found myself pacing the floor. I needed to talk to Juan to find out what he knew.

I decided the best thing to do would be to text him and ask him to call me when he was free. Just as I was getting ready to send my text, my phone rang. Since I was overseas my caller ID did not tell me who was calling.

"Hello, lovely. I have been missing you." Juan's voice was as smooth as ever. "How have you been getting along in Hoi An?"

"Oh Juan, I was just about to send you a text to ask you to call me. I have missed you also and I have many questions for you."

"Whoa, slow down. What has been going on?"

"I met with a friend of An's, who used to work at the plant where we are having the spring line made. She has been telling me about the changes at the plant. Are you aware that it is owned by a Chinese company?"

"Of course I am. That is why I am in Xiamen. This is where the company that owns the plant in Hoi An is based. They are a reputable firm with plants based all around the globe. Now what is it that An's friend told you that has you so upset?"

Something in his tone warned me not to share information that I had sourced through hearsay. "It seems she was laid off by this company and she said that there are rumors regarding the employees that are working in the plant."

"Well, I can totally vouch for the ethics of this company. Christine and I have been meeting with them for the past two days and everything that they have shown us seems to be of top quality. In addition, they can bring us this quality at very competitive prices."

"Have you heard anything about them setting up a demo shop to show prospective customers what they can do?"

"I have heard about this, but I can assure you that as your agent I would not support this selling practice. Now I hope that I have put all of your concerns out of your head.

Remember, you don't want to talk to individuals that have lost their jobs. They tend to be bitter and will not give you the business facts behind the decisions that have been made. I am just looking out for you and the last thing that I want for you is for you to go back home with more stories. I assured Clark that if you came over here that I would make sure that you stayed on track for what you needed to accomplish."

Something in his tone made me feel like a three-year-old. "I hear you. I assured Sandy that I would be focused on setting up the distribution plan. Am I going to see you before I go back?"

"That is why I was calling. It seems that Christine and I need to go to Shanghai to finish up the details of this deal. That will take another three days. It looks like I will not see you face to face until we meet again in Seattle."

This news both relieved and disappointed me. "I am sorry about that. I was looking forward to seeing you and talking about anything but work."

"Me too, but we will make up for it when I come back to Seattle. Now promise me you won't spend any more time talking to local rumor-mongers."

"Will do. Have a good trip."

After hanging up, I felt more confused instead of relief. What did he mean by saying that he would not support a demo shop when, it seems, that is exactly what happened on the last visit? I could not believe that Juan would mislead me, but the stories that I heard from Cam Le contradicted what Juan was saying.

Also, my stomach turned at the thought of Juan and Christine spending more time together in China. There was something about Juan that made me want to believe the best in him despite the growing number of contradictions. I knew that they were not at the plant the last time, so they had to have been visiting a demo site. Why would Juan lie to me? I also could not get past Christine misleading everyone about my whereabouts the last time I was in Hoi An.

I was still dealing with jet lag, and was wide awake as I was wrestling with all of these concerns. I decided the best thing to do was to add these questions to my check list so that before I left the country, I could resolve these issues. I owed it to my own sanity, as well as Darcy's, to get to the bottom of this dilemma.

Chapter 28

"You look like you did not sleep at all well last night. Was it the jet lag?" An's opening remarks made me realize that my efforts to camouflage my lack of shut-eye had not been successful. Maybe I should have taken those makeup lessons my sister was always trying to push on me.

"I talked to Juan last night," I said "and I am conflicted over what he told me."

"What was that? You didn't say anything about Cam Le, did you?"

"I mentioned her but not by name. And don't worry, when I heard that he was reacting so sternly about hearing anything negative regarding the plant, I immediately dropped the subject."

An did not seem reassured by this. "Reese, we promised her that anything she said would not get back to the owners of the plant. I think she does not trust them."

"I get it. My problem is that I don't know who to believe, Cam Le or Juan. I can't get the two different stories out of my head. I have to resolve this before I leave the country. The only way that I can think of finding out the absolute facts is to somehow visit the plant."

"But you saw the security at the gate. We had difficulties just driving by the location, so how do you think that we could get inside?"

"You mentioned that your brother was friends with the maintenance crew. What exactly do they do for the plant?"

"I am not really sure, but based on what they do for other facilities they go into the operation at night and do the janitorial service. Reese, what are you thinking?" An's face looked panic-stricken.

"Come on, An. It is the only way. I have to go in with the crew and find out once and for all what is going on. The best case would be that I find a perfectly well-run plant and I can chalk up Cam Le's comments to what Juan was saying— nothing more than rumblings from a disgruntled employee."

"But how can we do that? Notice I said 'we,' since I am not going to let you do this on your own. I owe it to Cam Le, and now to you, to find out the truth also."

An had no idea how relieved I was to hear her say that. Having her to help me with this would make it all possible. "Here's my idea. We convince Vinh to talk to his friend to let us be part of the janitorial crew. I was worried about how I was going to manage the language barrier but with you at my side I can just follow your lead."

"You mean we put on their uniforms and actually go with the crew inside the plant?"

"Yes, that is my plan."

"Leave Vinh to me. He is my baby brother and he has never refused me anything that I ask. He, like me, owes a lot to the support that the locals give my mother, so if we can find out what is truly going on in the plant, it is one way for us to clear up any false information that seems to be circulating in the community." An looked at her phone. "I am going to leave you now and go and find him. Let's meet for lunch at Mother's restaurant and we can work out the details for our escapade. Can you finish up the work here so that Juan doesn't become aware that we are not on task?"

"Yes," I said. "I will finish up everything here while you work things out. I am so relieved. I will see you at the restaurant at noon."

Chapter 29

I walked into the restaurant after a crazy taxi ride to get there. Since I had wanted An to have the time to meet with her brother alone, I had told them not to worry, that I would find my way to the restaurant on my own. Unlike my past adventures I actually arrived at the restaurant in one piece and on time. Maybe I was beginning to get the knack of this international travel.

I spied An, her brother and a third gentleman at a table in the far corner of the restaurant. An's mother rushed to greet me at the door. "I am so honored that you are back at my establishment. An said that you had business that you wanted to discuss with Vinh's friend Bao, so I have seated you in the far corner of the restaurant."

"Thank you very much, Kim-Ly." I followed her to the table. It seemed to be a secluded location, safe from eavesdropping. I was becoming paranoid given all of the conflicting information that I was uncovering.

As I approached the table, Vinh and his friend jumped to their feet. I love the politeness and respect in this country. "Reese, allow me to introduce my oldest friend in Hoi An, Bao Lee."

"Bao, it is an honor to meet you." I started to extend one hand and then I remembered that the normal protocol was to shake with both hands.

"The pleasure is all mine, Reese. Vinh and An have been telling me all about you and I am honored to make your acquaintance."

Kim-Ly had been hovering in the background as the introductions were taking place. "You must all eat my beautiful lunch first before talking business. I will bring you my famous spring rolls, a spinach salad and Ca Kho To, which means to you, Reese, a caramelized fish in a clay pot. It is one of the specialties of my restaurant, and was An and Vinh's father's favorite meal." She scurried away to the kitchen to place our order.

"Mother truly likes you, Reese," An said. "I can tell this because she is bringing out her favorite foods for you. This is her ultimate sign of respect."

I was very touched by this gesture. The idea of caramelized fish seemed a little strange, but as they say 'when in Rome do as the Romans do'.

Not wanting to be disrespectful I waited until we had finished a truly fantastic lunch. After lunch, I filled Bao in on our sleuthing adventure. "Bao, An tells me that your company does business with the manufacturing plant outside of town. What is it specifically that you do for them?"

"We are one of the few local companies that still does work for this plant. When the Chinese bought the business, they brought in all of their own labor except for a few of us. I guess their teams did not want to do the deep cleaning in the facility. We go into the plant once a week and do a thorough cleaning of the entire premises.

"Vinh has told me that you and An would like to accompany my team on our cleaning trip. He has not told me why, and I am curious as to why you would like to go with us?"

From the look An was sending me, this was not the time for total honesty. My objective was to get inside the plant and if I needed to tell a little white lie to accomplish this, so be it.

"My company is doing business with this plant and it is part of my job to ensure that the facility is in top condition. If I told them that I was visiting, it would not serve as an unannounced visit. However, if I could visit the plant with you, I could vouch for your performance as well as check the unannounced visit off of my checklist." I felt that was as close to the truth that I was capable of telling Bao. I could tell by the look of relief on An's and Vinh's faces that I had caught their unspoken message and passed the test.

"This account is very important to my business," Bao said. "However, from what you are saying, I do not see any problem with you visiting the facility with my crew. I will just add your names to the list of workers that we are required to give the company in advance. If you don't mind, Reese, I will change your name to a more Vietnamese-sounding name just to make sure that we do not raise suspicions."

"Good idea, Bao," An said. "How about the name Bian? I know that it means secretive. However, it is a very common name in this town, probably due to the past secrets during the American War." An always has a way to bring past history into the present.

"I like it. Reese, you now will be called Bian Le. We are scheduled to visit the plant tomorrow night so you will need to join our team at our offices at 9:00 p.m. An, I am sure that you will help Reese to dress the part. It would not be good for my team to be too suspicious of you. I will tell them that we were shorthanded and I asked An and you, An's cousin, to come and help out. As you know, after the American War, there were many Vietnamese children who have American fathers. I will tell them that you are from North Vietnam so that they will understand if you do not follow all of our local customs."

Chapter 30

An and I spent the following day finishing up the distribution plan and getting ready for our sleuthing adventure. Vinh brought us our uniforms: black pants, dark green smock tops with the embroidered BLC logo, tennis shoes and a green logo baseball caps.

"This cap is just what we need to camouflage your hair," An said. "I was worried how we were going to disguise your thick curly hair for tonight."

"Oh, I hadn't thought about that."

"It is very unusual to see a native Vietnamese with naturally curly hair. But with this cap you can put your hair into a top knot and keep it under the cap. You are built the same as me, so I think that I will not have any difficulty passing you off as my cousin."

That evening, Vinh drove us to within a block of the headquarters of Bao's business. "I am going to leave you off here so that you can walk into the office. If some of the other employees see you coming in a Mercedes they will wonder what is going on. Remember, you are just going into the plant to see what is going on. Do not take any unnecessary risks. I just do not trust the owners and I owe it to Bao to not have him lose this business based on your actions."

"You have told us this at least a hundred times since we started this plan yesterday," An said. "We've got it and I promise we will be careful."

With those parting words, An and I got out of the car and started our walk to the office. At least it was not raining even though the humidity was so high it felt like we were walking in the middle of a cloud. We entered a warehouse. We signed in with the receptionist on duty. I concentrated on signing my new name: Bian Le.

Bao spoke to the team in Vietnamese. I used all of my skills at watching body language and gestures to follow what was being said. Based on everyone turning toward An and me, I assumed that we were being introduced. I smiled and gave a small wave, imitating the same gesture that I saw An give to the team. We then followed behind the group toward the van that would take us to the plant.

Before I climbed into the van, Bao motioned to An and me. "It appears that everyone is relieved to have the extra help for the cleaning project tonight so they are not asking any questions about either of you. Just follow the instructions given to you by the crew lead and you should be fine. An, you will have to be subtle about how you give Reese information in English so as not to give away your disguise. Remember that even though everyone will be speaking in Vietnamese, the majority of this team will understand English if they overhear you talking."

With these less-than-encouraging instructions, Bao left us to join the crew. We were the last ones to get in the van. The crew consisted An, me and five others. There were three men and two young women, all in their early twenties. It appeared that the two women were attached with two of the men. The third man seemed happy to have two new women to entertain him. He began speaking quite rapidly to An and me. An responded in Vietnamese, turned her back on him, and spoke in low tones to me. "He asked me if you were with anyone and if you would like to go out after we finished

tonight. I told him that you were engaged and not available."
An's words seemed to have the necessary dampening effect on
my prospective suitor.

When we arrived at the plant the security guard looked
at his list on a clip board and compared it with the head count
in the van. When he was satisfied that the numbers matched
he gave the clip board to the lead of the crew. I was so
relieved that this was not the same guard that I had seen on
my first visit. Dao, the team lead, signed the clipboard and we
proceeded to drive to the entrance of the plant. Through all of
this my stomach was turning somersaults. I kept telling myself
just keep a neutral face. My only objective was to see the
inside of the plant and determine once and for all what was
going on.

Dao spoke to everyone inside the plant and gave out
work assignments. Thank goodness he gestured that An and I
would work together. I don't know what I would have done if
that hadn't happened. The building was a three story facility.
The first floor was a reception area and had what appeared to
be employee offices in the front of the building. Behind the

wall of offices I saw the shipping entrance to the plant. There was a conveyor belt that led from the second floor; I assumed that the boxes were sent down to be loaded on the trucks.

I followed An up some rickety iron steps placed in the back of the building to the second floor. This was a large room that was split in half; one half was set up with large tables and the other half of room with a number of old fashioned looking sewing machines. Low hanging neon lights draped over the various work stations. There were small windows around the perimeter of the room but they were covered with bars. I felt as I was in a prison and not a work facility.

"How can people work in this environment?" I whispered to An. I was having a hard time keeping the shock off of my face.

"Shh, Bian; someone will hear you. We are still supposed to go to the third floor and clean the restrooms. Obviously we are not getting any special treatment in terms of work assignments."

We walked through the manufacturing floor and found another set of rickety steps. As we started climbing up the stairs, I could hear noise coming from the third floor. "What do you think is going on? I thought everyone was supposed to be gone."

"I don't know but we will soon find out. Just keep your head down and focus on getting to work. Don't let anyone see your phone!"

I quickly put my phone back into the pocket of my smock. I had been taking pictures of the manufacturing floor just to prove to Sandy and Clark that the ideal manufacturing line they had seen was not the same one where the clothes were actually being manufactured.

On the third floor we could hear sewing machines operating behind closed doors. I wanted to get into that room but since our assignment was to clean the restrooms I reluctantly followed An to start our cleaning job.

When we entered the restroom An announced our arrival to anyone that may be inside. I was walking toward the rear of the long line of restroom stalls when I heard someone crying behind the last door. "Oh no," I thought; what should I do now? I gestured to An toward where the crying was coming from. An went to the door and spoke in Vietnamese to see if the person behind the door was okay. There was no response but the crying came to a stop. The next thing I saw the door slowly open and small girl came out of the stall. She was obviously not from Vietnam, but I could not determine where she was from. An went up to her and spoke to her in Vietnamese to see if she was okay. She obviously did not understand a word that An was saying. I then went up to her and began speaking in English "Are you okay? Can you understand English?"

She was very small and it was hard to determine her age. She had big brown eyes and long dark hair. Her skin tone appeared to be very tan. "I understand English. Who are you? The normal cleaning crew would not be up here."

"We are the normal cleaning crew and we were sent up to this floor to clean the restrooms. We were concerned when we heard you crying." I said.

"Oh I can't be seen talking to you. I just had to get away for a while and I came in here where the supervisor would not bother me."

"Why are you working at night?"

"We have a big project to finish. We have to ship these clothes to the States and we are behind schedule so we are all required to work all night until the project is finished."

"You did not understand Vietnamese when I spoke to you, where are you from?" An asked.

"I am here from the Philippines. My family lives in Manila and I miss them."

"Why are you here?" I asked.

"It is the custom in my family that when you turn sixteen that you go overseas to earn money to send back to the family. In many cases my sisters have found jobs on cruise ships but since I am afraid of being on the water, I thought I would work for this Chinese company doing what I have always done, making clothes. But it is terrible."

"What do you mean?"

"They told my parents that we would learn a trade and they would provide room and board in exchange for us working for them. However, when we got here they took our passports and we cannot leave the premises. I sit at a sewing machine twelve hours a day doing the same thing over and over. But I have talked too much and I need to get back to the line."

"Wait – what is your name?'

"I don't want to tell you. I have to keep this job." As she said that, she literally ran out of the restroom.

"What have we stumbled onto?" I looked at An, who had the same look of shock on her face as I did. The only smart thing I did was press the record button on my phone while she was telling us her story.

"Let's finish cleaning these restrooms and get out of here" An said.

"I agree."

We then did the fastest cleaning of toilets possible. Since the water was rusty and the porcelain was old, no amount of scrubbing would make much of a change, which made for a very quick cleaning job. We gathered up our supplies and headed for the rickety steps back down stairs. Just when we had reached the steps the door opened to the room where everyone was working. A short stocky Chinese gentleman yelled at us in Vietnamese. We stopped in our tracks and An turned and faced him. He began gesturing to the inside of the room. An walked to the room and I followed in her footsteps.

Inside the room we saw at least 20 women sitting at sewing machines. They had their heads down, looking at the bright colored fabric they were working on. The Chinese gentleman handed us two brooms and made the gesture that he wanted the floors swept. These floors looked like they had not been swept in years. Besides thread and fabric strewn everywhere there was dust and dead cockroaches mixed in the mess. I was getting sick to my stomach just looking at it all.

An whispered to me "Just keep it together and let's clean up these floors. The supervisor said that he did not want the women to take a break to clean but even he knew that these floors were a health hazard."

I noticed at the back of the room was the little Filipino girl that we had talked to in the restroom. She, more than the rest, did not look at us as we began the sweeping project. An took the east side of the room and I used the push broom down the west side. I wished I had a face mask on while I was pushing through all the dust and grime.

After about twenty minutes, we had large piles of trash by the door. We took two of our trash bags and literally shoveled the debris into the bags. The Chinese gentleman grunted his approval as he abruptly turned and made an exit.

As we finished piling up the bags, I noticed a table in the corner that had several of the tops that the women had been making. I felt like I had struck the jackpot. These tops were the ones for the spring line for Darcy's. After a quick glance to see that no eyes were on me, I grabbed one and stuffed it in my jacket. Just when I had finished this the supervisor came back into the room. He immediately went over to the pile of tops and began to count them. He made a gesture that indicated that the team had not produced enough tops. I knew that if we did not get out of that room quickly someone would tell him about the top that I had taken. I really needed this item to prove to Sandy and Clark about what was going on in this plant.

Throughout this entire procedure not one person in that room spoke or stopped working. I felt that I had been in a room with human robots except that robots would probably have had better machines to work on. An and I lugged the bags out of the room and down the stairs to the dumpster. Dao met us at the base of the stairs pointedly looking at his watch. When he saw us bringing the large bags of trash he shrugged his shoulders and called two of the guys over to help us carry our bundles out of the plant.

I felt like I was covered in dust and grime. I knew one thing for sure; if I lost my job at Darcy's I definitely was not going to apply to work for a manufacturing janitorial service. Just when we were ready to leave I saw the fat guard who had confronted me the first time. It appeared that he was inspecting everyone when they were leaving the building. This could be trouble since not only could he recognize me, but also I still had that shirt hidden in my pants under the smock.

I whispered to An "I have to get out of here without having him inspect me. He's the one that chased me away the first time"

An looked at me with a panic stricken face "What are we going to do?"

We were standing on the main floor. "Here let's go to the back of the building" While the guard was giving Dao a thorough going over and starting to look in the bags of trash that they were hauling out An and I darted to the back of the building on the main floor. We went into an office at the farthest point in the rear. "An, you have to go out there and stand in line for your exit search. I have to get this top out of the building so I will figure out another way to camouflage it and then join you."

"Be careful" An said as she left me to walk to the exit.

I heard Dao speaking to the guard. I had no idea what was being said but I had just enough time to thoroughly hide the top in my pants. I knew I needed to get out there before I raised any more suspicion with the guard. I knew I looked totally different from when I saw him the first time but I still had the image of that gun in my head.

I slowly walked toward the entrance grasping my stomach as if I was in pain. Dao looked at me in concern and started speaking to me in Vietnamese. I just clutched my stomach and bent forward. An came running back to me and put her arm around my shoulder to assist me. She said something to Dao and the guard and I just continued to grab my stomach and bend forward. It worked the guard couldn't get me out of the building fast enough.

I sat in the van for the entire trip back to the office just moaning and clutching my prize around my stomach. I couldn't get away from these people fast enough. It was definitely time for me to return to Seattle.

Chapter 31

I was thankful that this trip was only two flights instead of three; I guess that's what planning is for. Of course, I didn't plan on the delay in my flight out of Da Nang and now I was stressing about getting to Seoul in time for my connecting flight home. I was hoping to use the four hours to get organized about how I was going to share all that I had collected with Clark and Sandy, not worry about if I'd get home easily. Such a glamorous life I lead!

We finally boarded the plane and we were ready to leave the gate when the flight attendant announced that we would depart in 30 minutes, after all the baggage was loaded on to the plane. They offered beverages, so I had a glass of wine as a way to calm my nerves. Of course, the minute we took off, I fell into a deep sleep, waking up just as we were landing in Seoul. Somehow, we made up time in the air and I had two hours before my flight home.

The last time I flew home, I had no time at Incheon Airport and had no concept of the shopping there! I started wandering, drooling over the shoes at Ferragamo and the dresses at Paul Smith. I had no business even looking, let alone trying them on; but I did anyway. I kept thinking about Juan and what he'd like to see me in if I ever actually saw him again. I felt like a kid in a candy store as I wandered past Burberry, Cartier and Gucci.

I suddenly realized I was starving and decided to grab some sushi from Food on Air Studio 1. As I was paying the check, I realized I would now have to run to make my flight! Luckily, I wasn't as far from the gate as I thought and I joined the end of the boarding line as it was thinning out. Safely in my seat, I decided it was time to focus. The fun was over and now it was time to get to work. I took a few deep breaths to settle myself down from running down hallways, found my legal pad, took out my tray table and started to make some notes.

The flight was incredibly bumpy, making it hard to concentrate, let alone write. As it seemed to get worse, the pilot came over the loudspeaker to tell us that we would be in turbulent air for the next hour or so and that he was seating the flight attendants. This did not make me happy and I could sense tension in the passengers around me. I kept looking at my watch, hoping the hands would move faster instead of nearly sitting still.

It was more than an hour later when the flight attendants finally rose from their jump seats. It was still bumpy but I took that as a sign of calmer air to come. When things did calm down, I reset my desk and started to write. I created a timeline for the trip and then filled in the details. I filtered some things out, as I didn't think Clark or Sandy would care what we ate for dinner or lunch. I was familiar with Clark's short attention span, so I thought it would be better to stick to the facts without adding color or trying to draw conclusions.

I got through the first two days before meal service began. I couldn't believe I was hungry again, but I was. I put my notes away and ate while I watched a movie. I could feel myself nodding off and I didn't want to sleep, so when the movie ended I drank a big cup of coffee with sugar so I'd stay awake.

It took me nearly two more hours to complete the timeline and detailed notes, and I was feeling good about the end product. That said, I had no idea how Clark and Sandy would react, and I knew I was going to need time to practice before I made my presentation. I decided not to worry about it too much, as I expected it to be days before they actually set the meeting.

I had time for one more movie and opted for Batman. I remember my dad talking about the television show, but it was off the air by the time I was a kid. It was entertaining and action packed, which kept me awake for the duration of the flight.

Chapter 32

The sun was shining as we made our descent into Seattle. Our approach was from the south and out of my window I could almost see the Olympic Mountains, it was so clear. It is days like this that I am so glad I moved to the Pacific Northwest...there was still snow on the ground in North Dakota and here it was all shades of green.

I got through customs fairly easily and headed for the cab stand. As soon as we left the garage, I opened the back windows to take in the fresh, clean air. I was happy to be home but I had to admit that I missed An a bit. I felt like we were partners in this and it was strange to think we were miles apart. I meant to tell her that I hope we get to work together again soon. I'd just have to send her an email when I get to work.

I got home and unpacked, assessed the laundry pile and decided to throw in a load while I went through my mail. It was mostly catalogues and I enjoyed looking at some of the new fashions for summer. I put the wet clothes in the dryer, sat on the couch and took out the legal pad with my trip notes.

I was feeling extremely antsy as I was reading what I'd written; I think it was part exhaustion, part confusion and part disbelief. But there was a deeper, gnawing feeling that I couldn't quite identify, as if some of the pieces didn't fit. "Maybe fresh air will help," I thought; I grabbed my jacket and headed toward the waterfront.

Before I realized it, I was near the Edgewater hotel, famous for having been the place where Beatles stayed when they played in Seattle. The hotel literally sits out on a dock over the water, with an amazing view of Alki Beach. In one my history lessons from Dan, he told me that Seattle was founded by a landing on Alki Beach. He'd be proud that I remembered that.

The building looks like a log cabin and the lobby reminds me of hunting lodges I saw as a kid growing up in the Midwest. There was a roaring fire and a few animal heads mounted on the wall. It had a funny way of calming me down and the smell of food from the restaurant was making me hungry.

After all of the amazing food I had in Vietnam, I was craving noodles and red sauce, and a big glass of red wine, Carmine style Carmine's was my next stop. As I walked back toward Pioneer Square, I thought about how lucky I was to have Carmine as a friend. We had this instant connection that confused me at first because I couldn't understand why he was so nice to me. I guess he sensed that because he told me about how much I reminded of his niece.

"You remind me so much of my niece, Alexa. She moved to New York when she was about your age. She lost her dad when she was twelve and I promised my sister I would do what I could to help her raise Alexa. She brought me more joy than I could have imagined and I miss her terribly."

From that moment on, I knew I could count on Carmine to be there if I needed him. Jack and Carey are great friends, too; but Carmine is also a mentor in ways that they can't be.

I took a seat at the bar. Carmine was in a great mood, came around from behind the bar and gave me a big hug, which I realized I needed. I told him I'd returned from Vietnam earlier in the day and was craving the basic stuff. Within seconds, the glass of wine was in front of me, along with a small plate of prosciutto and fresh burrata. I sometimes forget that these are Italian basics!

It was rather quiet, perhaps because it was early, and Carmine took the time to sit with me and ask about my trip. I tried to dance around the big stuff, but as he always does, went straight to the point.

"What's troubling you, Reese?"

I looked around the restaurant to be sure there were no familiar faces and then told him the gist of what I'd seen and what I thought it meant. I left out the parts about Juan, but he kept digging.

"Is that all?"

I couldn't lie to him, and I guess I have a bad poker face.

"The agent in Vietnam was in Seattle a few weeks ago and we had dinner together." I told him the rest of the story, embarrassing as it was.

More silence.

"Somehow, he managed to arrange a trip for me to come back to Vietnam, but when I got there, he told me he had to go to China instead. While he was in China, I asked him about the conversation I had with Cam Le and what I'd seen at the factory and he dismissed it. I'm confused, but I really do believe him."

Carmine scowled. "Well, I worry less about his role in this and more about your obvious attraction to him. He's older, lives in another country and does business with your employer. I don't see how any of this is good."

I was a little miffed that he was so quick to condemn Juan, but everything he said was factual, not judgmental. The wine had gone to my head and I simply said, "I don't know what it is, but there is something about this man and I know it's mutual."

I immediately realized that was throwing fuel on the fire, but Carmine is all about respect. He simply said, "As I told Alexa when she went to the big city, make sure your head and heart are always in balance. You are smart but also still young, and some people take advantage of that."

With that, he walked into the kitchen and brought me a beautiful bowl of linguini with red sauce. He stayed behind the counter but took my hands and said, "Enjoy your dinner and keep your head on straight." With that, he disappeared into the kitchen and barked in Italian to the prep cooks.

Chapter 33

The office was quiet when I walked in Monday morning. Jason told me that Sandy was home sick, Christine was still out of town and it had been pretty quiet overall. I was dreading opening my email, fearing an overload, but I got through them in about an hour.

As I was about to go to a different screen and settle into work, an email from Juan popped up: *I'm in Seattle to take you to dinner and make up for having to go to China. No business this trip. Casual evening; please give me your address and I'll pick you up at 7:00. J.*

A big smile came over my face. This convinced me that I meant something to him, which confirmed to me that he was being honest. I wasn't sure how I'd work the rest of the day, but I did. And got home just in time to take a shower and put together something casual but elegant. As I turned the corner at the top of the stairs to go to my front door, I saw a large bouquet of flowers. I dropped my purse as I leaned over to pick up the card: *See you at 7; can't wait. J.*

Chapter 34

I took a quick shower, tried to style my wild and unruly hair, and tried on almost every outfit I could come up with to find the perfect one. I settled for a pair of lavender corduroy pants, a purple sweater and a pair of short, black leather boots that mom gave me as a birthday gift last year. While I was in Vietnam, I bought a simple but beautiful silk scarf that worked perfectly with my sweater. Even so, I wasn't sure my heart would stay in my chest as I waited impatiently for 7:00 p.m.

Just as I was calming down, there was a knock on my door; through the peephole I could see his handsome face, which made my heart race all over again. I opened the door and we immediately embraced as if it had been months, not days, since we'd seen each other. Just looking at him made me feel like lightning was running through my veins and I wondered how I was going to handle another dinner with him.

He helped me into my coat. "I have a car waiting downstairs and we have a reservation at 7:30. Let's go."

The driver opened the car door for us, and Juan followed me in. I saw the bucket that had champagne on ice, but I tried not to act like a curious kid by staring at it. As the driver went up front, Juan opened a cabinet and pulled out two champagne flutes, and poured us each a glass. "To us on this beautiful evening," he said. I was smitten.

We went to Madison Valley, a relaxed but upscale neighborhood east of downtown that I'd never been to before. The car stopped in front of a warm and inviting little French restaurant, the likes of which I'd not seen before. Juan had brought a bottle of wine, which he gave to the hostess, and we were taken to a quiet little table in the window that looked out on a small garden. The aromas were intoxicating, which just heightened every single feeling going on in my head and my body. I thought the champagne would calm me down, but I was wrong.

We had smoked salmon tartine to start, as well as the salade Lyonnaise to follow the Northwest bouillabaisse main course. The tartine arrived just as Juan made another toast: "To Darcy's, for putting us together."

For some reason, that struck me as odd because I think of Juan so differently than I do someone from work, but I let it pass. He made a point of saying that he was here for a few days of rest after weeks of hard work, and that he couldn't think of a better way than starting off the time with me. I was flattered.

The bouillabaisse arrived and our server carefully dished it out to be sure we had the right balance of broth and seafood. Juan poured more wine, which tasted even better with the food. There was so much going on in my mouth—the richness of the seafood, the sweetness of the tomato broth and the earthiness of the wine. I was definitely going to have to tell Carmine about this place!

Dinner flew by as we talked about my childhood in North Dakota, what brought me to the Pacific Northwest and finally, what I thought about Seattle. Juan asked so many questions that, when the salad arrived, I realized hadn't had a chance to ask him much at all. "Juan, I've been doing all the talking tonight. I want to know about your life, too."

"It's really not that exciting and I'm much more interested in learning about you. But you're right, I haven't said much. I'm the child of a career military family; my father met my mother while he was stationed in Fort Ord. My mom worked in her family's restaurant in Carmel, which he frequented when he had time off. They say it was love at first sight and while she hated to have to leave Carmel when he was transferred, they were in love. I was born two years after they married."

His description of his parents brought a smile to my face. It sounded as if he had a lot of love growing up.

"Although my father came from a long line of military, I had no interest. He said that was fine as long as I got a good education and became a successful businessman. I went off to college and then business school. College is where I first met Clark."

"I found my way into the clothing business just as manufacturing was becoming big business in Vietnam. Maybe it's because we moved a bit as I grew up, but I had this incredible desire to visit Asia, so I found a job with a company that was also doing business in Vietnam. I worked my way up the ladder until I had enough management experience to open and run facilities in Vietnam."

I was struck by how motivated he was in business, maybe money. This was so different than how my parents were in the retail world.

"Once I got there, I saw even greater opportunity to work as an agent, bringing together deals between U.S. retailers and Vietnamese manufacturers. And here I am."

I was impressed. "Juan, that's such a motivating story. You knew what you didn't want, which led you to what you want."

With that, he took both my hands in his and said, "I do know what I want, yes. Right now, I want you."

As if on cue, the check arrived and Juan slipped the server his credit card. Meanwhile, my head was spinning and I was both terrified and excited. No one has ever said those words to me before. I was almost speechless, but managed to choke out a "thank you."

Juan must have sensed my surprise, as he looked into my eyes and said, "Reese, you have been a mystery to me since we met and I want to know you better—it's that simple."

I collected myself as we stepped back into the car for our short ride home. It suddenly occurred to me that I had no idea what was coming next. I knew I didn't want the night to end, but I wasn't sure what to do.

"Reese, you're far away. What are you thinking?"

"I was just reflecting on what an amazing meal that was, and I really enjoyed hearing about your life."

"Well, we're not done yet. We have champagne to finish at your loft, if that's okay with you."

Okay with me? Who was he kidding? This man was like no other and despite warnings from Jack and Carmine, I was not going to worry about Vietnam, Darcy's or anything other than Juan and me. "It's perfect."

Chapter 35

The car dropped us off at my loft. I got out and as Juan did the same, he said something to the driver that I couldn't quite hear. He carried the bottle of champagne and the two flutes as we walked slowly up the stairs.

It was chilly in my apartment, so I turned up the heat while Juan rinsed and dried the flutes, and poured us each a glass of champagne. We sat on the couch and I managed to propose the toast this time: "To you, for a wonderful evening."

"One that is not over yet," he added.

We sipped our champagne until the glass was empty, mostly in silence, but somewhat quickly. Juan asked if I'd like more and I declined. While he was in Seattle to relax, I had to be at work and ready at any moment to give my report to Clark and Sandy.

As if he sensed I was thinking about work, he gently held my face in his hands and began to kiss me ever so slowly. I literally melted into his arms as he drew me closer to him. I could feel his heart beating and my desire for him was incredibly strong. "Reese, you are so beautiful and I am incredibly attracted to all of you. I feel as if I want to please you in any way I can, if you'll let me."

At that point, I felt completely under his spell and all I wanted was him. He began kissing my neck, gently untying and removing my scarf. The feel of his lips were incredible, soft and warm, but commanding at the same time. As he was kissing me, I fell easily onto the couch, pulling him toward me. While he resisted, it was only so that he could untuck my sweater. He lifted me gently and slipped it off as I started to unbutton his shirt. We were looking at each other in this moment, but I was too starry eyed to read anything in his expression.

He was an exquisite man and I had never been with anyone like him before. As nervous as I had been, nothing ever felt better or more natural to me. I tried to reach behind me to turn off the light, but he grabbed my hand and whispered, "I want to be able to see you."

I closed my eyes, as if I wanted to be surprised by what would happen next. He gently kissed my neck, then my breasts as he unzipped my pants. I was incredibly aroused at this and

251

began moving my hips in response to his touch. I was trying to grab at his belt but I didn't have the coordination to get there in this state. He laid himself gently on top of me, moving in rhythm. I could feel him, hard as a rock, and I wasn't sure if I could contain myself. I pulled him closer to me and whispered, "Let's go to bed."

We both slipped out our pants before we left the living room. I couldn't help but stare at him as I removed his boxer shorts.

"I'll remove yours in bed, my way," he said, as we walked the five steps into the bedroom. He sat me on the bed and knelt before me. "I want us to make love tonight, slowly and sweetly, if that's okay with you."

"Juan, I am yours." I laid back and let him remove my panties. As he moved his hands down my legs, he gently spread me open, teasing me with his tongue. I could feel an orgasm brewing, so I took a deep breath and went with it. At that moment, he entered me with a comfortable force that made me moan loudly. We began to kiss as we moved in tandem, stopping at times as if to slow the process down. This only heightened the feeling and I couldn't hold on anymore.

I whispered, "I'm ready for you," and we thrust harder at each other, enjoying the release and sensitivity that followed after we both came.

We both lay there, holding each other tightly, breathing slowly as if we were trying to get our heart rates to slow. We turned on our side, still connected. "Reese, you are exquisite. Smart, beautiful and incredibly sensual."

He forgot shy, which was how I felt when he said this to me. I have never been great at talking about sex even with my girlfriends, let alone a man. I couldn't find any words, so I simply smiled at him and then kissed him again. I really loved kissing this man and he seemed to enjoy it, too.

When we finally disconnected, he pulled the covers over us and asked me how I was feeling.

"I feel amazing, relaxed and electrified," I said. "You are incredible and make me feel things I've never felt before."

I could see from the light from the moon pouring in the window that he was smiling. We both laid there for a while in silence, but soon I could feel my increasing desire for him once again. I turned toward him and began to kiss his chest and that was all it took for us to make love again before we fell asleep in each other's' arms.

I heard the shower running as my alarm went off. I jumped out of bed and joined him there. It was fun and playful, as we snuck in kisses while playing games with the soap. I didn't have much time to play, so I jumped out of the shower to dry my hair and get dressed.

"I'll have the car here to take you to work before I'm dropped off at the hotel. The driver will stop for coffee on his way; how do you take it?"

I could get used to this. "Short half-caf latte. Thank you, Juan."

Fifteen minutes later we were in the car with coffees and delicious almond stuffed croissants from a French bakery on Capitol Hill. We arrived at my building too quickly and I really wasn't ready to go to work, much preferring to stay in this bubble for the rest of the day.

"Reese," Juan said, "I'm going to my hotel and then going to see an old family friend who lives in Vancouver. I'll be back late this evening and will call you tomorrow morning. I enjoyed last evening and look forward to seeing you again."

While this felt awkward, I understood he had a life and we did have an amazing evening. "Thank you, Juan, for a beautiful night. Have a great time in Vancouver and I'll speak to you in the morning."

He kissed me gently and said goodbye as I got out of the car and slowly walked up to my office. The lights in Christine's office were still off, but clearly Sandy was in because I heard her voice on the phone. Jason gave me a sleepy nod as I got settled at my desk.

Chapter 36

I tried to focus on my e-mails but I could not get last night out of my head. I heard Jason's voice calling to me: "Reese, wake up, you are just staring at your computer. What did you do last night? Obviously something more fun than going to swim lessons with a five- and seven-year old."

"Oh sorry. I guess I was lost in thought and the jet lag from my trip was catching up with me. What has been going on here since I have been away?"

"The noise from the clothing-return fiasco from Christmas seems to have slowed down. Sarah is pushing for Clark to rescind his money-back-guarantee program before the spring launch. Somehow I think she is fighting a losing battle, as you know how Clark gets when he is focused on implementing one of his ideas."

Just then I saw an e-mail pop up on my screen. I was invited to meet tomorrow with Clark and Sandy to recap the distribution strategy. My stomach immediately began turning somersaults.

"Well, it looks like I have an audience with Clark tomorrow to talk about my trip to Vietnam. Any words of advice for me when I make this presentation?"

"Just keep it short and fact-based. It would be great if you had some visuals, as you know Clark is a very visually-based person. I can't imagine them spending much time with you. Clark is not famous for spending much time worrying about the details. He will be already thinking about his next idea. If Bill is there, he will want to know the details but that conversation may happen outside of the meeting."

Just then Sarah came up to us. "Reese, that cute agent from Vietnam is back. I just saw him walking into Clark's office."

"You mean Juan."

"Yes, I guess that is his name. I just have his beautiful face permanently etched on my brain."

How well I could identify with that statement. But what was Juan doing in Clark's office? I thought he was on vacation and off to Vancouver.

"Is Christine here?" I asked.

"She should be in shortly. She just got back in town last night also," Jason said.

I decided before I worked on my presentation any more I needed to see if I could figure out why Juan was in the building. I could not believe that after our wonderful night, Juan would mislead me as to his real plans for the day. "Sorry, guys, but I need to meet with Harry and talk to him regarding the final details regarding the distribution plan." I grabbed my notebook, almost knocking over my chair, and left Sarah and Jason staring at my frenzy.

I did need to talk to Harry, but I thought I would walk by Clark's office on my way to the fourth floor. His office is sheltered by his admin's cubicle but I would be able to see through the glass partition if a certain someone was in the area.

Bill's office is next to Clark's. One of the many lessons I learned from Jason after coming to the corporate office was to become good friends with the administrative assistants. They controlled the schedules of their bosses and were an excellent source of information.

I had befriended Kay, who was Bill's admin. She was also from a small town in the Midwest and was getting used to living in a "big city." Her husband had been transferred here by Amazon, so I could always be entertained by the latest office gossip he brought home from that corporation.

"Reese, good to see you. How has life been on the international circuit?"

"Well, other than the jet lag it has been quite the adventure."

"I bet it has been. We have to go out so that you can entertain me with all of your stories."

As I was talking to Kay, I was looking over at Clark's office. She noticed that I was distracted. "You must have heard about the good-looking guy who is in Clark's office," she said with a smile. "I have to admit he has eyes that make you want to swoon."

"Christine said something about him being here. His name is Juan Gomez and he is the agent we are working with in Vietnam. So he is in Clark's office?"

"Yes I guess he is here to talk about some future buying deals. I really don't know what is going on. The only reason I know that much is that I have been covering for Jane, Clark's admin, while she is at the dentist."

"Oh. I did not know Juan was going to be in the office today. Oh well, I guess he does not need to check in with me." I headed off to Harry's office on the fourth floor.

Harry was, as usual, surrounded by reams and reams of paper. "Look at who is back in the good old USA."

"Hi, I thought I would stop by and see if anything new has happened since I was away."

"I just got the invite to come to your debrief regarding the distribution strategy tomorrow. Good luck with that. I have never seen Clark sit still through that type of detailed meeting."

"It seems like everyone is telling me that."

"Yes, especially since they have already made plans to expand the relationship with that supplier for the fall line of clothes."

"What? I did not know about that!"

"Yes I just got the e-mail from Christine today that Clark is meeting with his pal Juan and is going to agree to expand the relationship with this supplier for the fall line. I am really nervous about putting so much business in the hands of one agent and one supplier, but I guess that is why I don't get paid the big bucks."

After hearing this news my head was spinning. Had I been played? And for what? One thing was for certain—I needed to review my presentation and lay out all of the facts for management to assess.

I was working on autopilot for the rest of the day. I could not get it out of my head that Juan had misled me about his reasons for being in Seattle. What else was he keeping from me?

As I gathered up my purse and laptop to leave for the day, I noticed that Christine was just about to go into her office. It would probably be smart to see how she was doing before I had to deal with her tomorrow.

I walked to her office and stuck my head in the door.

"Welcome back. How was your trip?"

"Oh, hi, Reese. It was a good trip. I always have fun traveling with Juan in Asia. He knows everyone."

"Did you do the deal in Shanghai for the fall line?"

"Of course. With all of the success we are having with the pricing on the spring line we definitely need to expand this partnership. I received the invite to your presentation tomorrow. I can't believe that Sandy and Clark are wasting their time to talk to you about distribution. I hope you plan on keeping the meeting short. They are probably only talking to you to assess whether or not it was important to send someone over from the company to assist Juan with the details."

"You are probably right," I managed to say, but inside I was reeling. "Glad you had a good trip and I will see you tomorrow." I needed to leave the office immediately before I punched someone out. I could not believe the arrogance of Christine. *It will be interesting and enjoyable to see her reaction to my photos tomorrow.*

Chapter 37

I spent the evening downloading the pictures from my plant tour onto my laptop. As they always say, a picture speaks a thousand words. At about ten p.m., I received a call on my cell. I saw that the caller was not identified but I thought that it might be Juan.

"Hi, sweetie. I thought I would check in and see how your day went."

"Just work and getting caught up after being away. How was your trip to Vancouver?"

"It was just fine. I made some new contacts for future business. Clark tells me that you are making your distribution presentation tomorrow."

"Oh, did you talk to Clark?"

"Just by phone. He wanted me to stop by tomorrow to hear your presentation so I thought I would let you know that I will be in your meeting."

"This meeting keeps getting larger and larger. Christine told me she was going to be there and Harry from procurement is also going to be in attendance. I guess when Clark is in a meeting everyone wants to have a seat at the table with him."

"I guess so," he said. "I will leave the company politics to you. This is why I am glad that I work for myself. Reese, if you could do me a favor, and see if you could push Harry along to finish the paperwork on both this deal and future deals. I need to have the documents signed so that everything can continue to progress in a timely manner."

At this point I realized that what Jack, Carey and Carmine were telling me was true. Juan was definitely a smooth operator. I began to have this sense that he was just using me as another source for information at Darcy's.

"I really don't have much sway with Harry. But if you are at the meeting tomorrow you can talk to him yourself. Glad your trip to Vancouver went well." I really could not talk to him any longer. I politely ended the call, even though I wanted an old-fashioned phone that would let me slam the receiver down in his ear.

Chapter 38

After a sleepless night in which I saw each and every hour pass on the clock, I took my time getting ready for work. I wanted to wear my most professional look. I pulled out my tried-and-true black slacks, wine-colored blouse and long black cardigan sweater. I put on the silver necklace that was my graduation gift from my parents, for good luck. For once my unruly hair cooperated and I was able to craft it into a bun at the nape of my neck. After applying mascara and lip gloss I decided I at least looked the part.

I sat at my cube at 8:00 and decided all I had to do was not lose it before the meeting. Nine o'clock finally came, and I was in the conference room with enough butterflies in my stomach to stock a sanctuary. I hoped I could get my nerves under control so that I could gracefully deliver the presentation. Since Clark was going to be there, we were in the conference room right next to his office rather than the marketing conference room. This room added to my nervousness, since I knew it was where all of the company board meetings took place.

Everyone filed into the room right on time – Harry, Christine and Bill. "Reese, I hope you don't mind me crashing your meeting. I wanted to hear all about the distribution plans after your trip to Vietnam."

"No problem, Bill. I am glad you are here."

I heard laughter from the hall as Sandy, Clark and Juan entered the room. "Hi, everyone," Clark said. "I want you meet Juan Gomez, who has been responsible for setting up our sourcing plan in Vietnam. Juan, I assume you know most of everyone here."

"I haven't had the opportunity to meet Harry or Bill yet but it is great to be here," Juan as usual was as smooth as ever. All the handshaking took place while Clark took his customary place at the head of the conference table. "Now, Reese, tell us the distribution plan for the spring line. Then I want Juan and Christine to tell us about their plans for the fall line."

I opened my laptop, and my Power Point presentation. I was glad I had been in the room early so that I knew my presentation would project on the screen in the room.

The first picture I showed was the outside of the plant. "When I was in Vietnam," I began, "I was still concerned about the facility that I had visited based on the address given to me by Harry versus the location that you and Sandy visited three weeks ago. This is a picture of that location. When I spoke to the locals in Hoi An, I verified that this was in fact the plant where the clothing was manufactured."

"This can't be right. Reese, you are mistaken again," Christine said.

"Christine, let Reese continue," Clark said with authority.

"I interviewed past employees of the plant and found out that ever since the Chinese bought this facility, all of the local employees were released from duty and 'outsiders' were brought in to staff the plant. Notice the building behind the plant, which is dormitory where these employees live."

"I don't understand. We did not see any of this on our tour of the plant." Sandy seemed genuinely puzzled by my information.

"I understand, Sandy, and I was equally puzzled as to what was really happening. It appears that it is common practice for a manufacturer to set up a demo site to show to prospective customers that is totally compliant with the customer's requirements. When I spoke to An Le, who was my interpreter in Vietnam, she assumed that that is what had happened. I specifically asked Juan if this was the case and he stated that he was aware of this practice but would never be party to it."

"And I absolutely would not be party to this," Juan said vehemently. "I am as surprised by all of this as the rest of you."

"All right, let Reese finish," Clark said.

"When I heard this practice I knew that in spite of the orders from Juan to not go to the plant, I needed to get inside the facility and see what was going on. An and I went to the plant as part of the cleaning crew so that we could get an unbiased view as to the goings-on in the plant." I showed them the pictures of the entire cleaning crew, and explained how An and Vinh's relationship with the company allowed us to gain access.

"I have to admit, Reese that was very clever. What did you find out?"

"Clark, I want to warn you that you will not be happy with the results of my visit. I will let this recording speak for itself."

I then played the recording with the young girl from the Philippines. Clark's face was turning red while Sandy seemed to have lost all of the color in her face.

"Luckily, I was able to procure a sample of the clothing that is being made when we were cleaning the manufacturing area. I brought this sample back with me so that you could see the quality problems that are inherent with the manufacturing process." I passed the spring blouse to the team.

Clark looked at Christine and Juan. "What is going on? Is someone making money off of us while potentially ruining our reputation with our customers?"

"Clark, I am as much in the dark by all of this as you are but I will get to the bottom of it." Juan was getting red in the face.

"Juan, I hold you accountable for all of this," Clark said. Right now, everyone needs to leave the room and let Sandy, Bill and I sort this out. Harry, I want you to make sure you stop all contracts immediately with this firm until we find out what is going on."

"Yes sir," Harry said.

I could not look Juan in the eye. His lies were more than I could take.

"Reese, please email your presentation to the three of us to review. Bill, you need to call Security and legal to join our meeting."

With that said we filed out of the room. I walked as fast as possible to get away from Juan and Christine. I noticed that Juan was already on his phone.

When I got back to my desk, Jason looked at me. "What happened? Your face is as white as a ghost."

"I can't talk about it but it was not a meeting I would want anyone else to have to attend."

Christine came to my desk. "I can't believe you did that without talking to me. You just don't understand what it takes to do a deal in this environment. You are just a naïve Midwest girl that doesn't know how the real world works." With that she spun on her heel and left me and the building.

Epilog

What followed after a thorough investigation of the "fiasco" in Vietnam was not pretty. Christine was fired. Investigation revealed that she was taking kickbacks from the manufacturers to help her pay off her student-loan debt—and support her shopaholic tendencies.

While it was never proven whether Juan really knew what was going on, the company immediately severed the agency agreement with him—it was impossible that he didn't know, and his deceptions with me only reinforce that. To date, I have not heard anything more from him but the memories of our night together are both painful and sweet.

Clark personally reported the labor practices at the plant in Hoi An to the Vietnamese labor council. The Vietnamese, to their credit, stood up to the Chinese and evicted that management from the country. Meanwhile, an entrepreneur from Vietnam bought the plant at a discount and began employing the locals at the manufacturing site once again.

With full support from Harry and Sandy, An Le, my partner in uncovering all this mess, was given the opportunity to take over the agency relationship with Darcy's in Asia.

Sandy promoted me to Christine's position as the buying manager for the women's clothing line. Together with my buddy Jason, and with support from Sarah, we were able to replace in the entire spring line in a relatively short time and still have a spring promotion in the stores before summer came.

Now all I have to worry about is holiday!

Krista Fuller

Krista Fuller and KMF Consulting assist multi-unit retailers in developing their store development strategies for real estate acquisition, construction, design and maintenance. Prior to forming KMF Consulting, Krista was Senior Vice President of Business Development for First Service Networks; Krista worked for more than 30 years in executive roles with both Starbucks and 7-Eleven ranging from overall responsibility for the operations of the 7-Eleven stores across Canada, to maintaining and launching new markets for Starbucks coffeehouses in domestic and International marketplaces. These years of experience, extensive international travel and the people she met motivated Krista to co-author *Ladder Up.*

Audrey Lincoff

Audrey Lincoff is an award winning communications professional with more than 20 years' experience building corporate communications and consumer programs, and guiding initiatives for Fortune 500 companies in retail, hospitality and manufacturing industries among others. She currently leads Corporate Communications for a local, privately held asset management company. She served as vice president, Global Communications for Starbucks Coffee Company; vice president, Corporate Communications for Expedia, Inc., and senior vice president for Publicis Consultants USA (now MSL Group Seattle). Audrey's move to Seattle followed by her diverse experience in the corporate world and the desire to laugh inspired her to co-author *Ladder Up.*

Made in the USA
Las Vegas, NV
23 March 2022